# THE MYSTERIOUS MAN,

## OR THE THREE IN ONE.

### BEAUTIFULLY ILLUSTRATED BY PROWSE & WEBBE.

WILL BE COMPLETED

IN ABOUT 20 NUMBERS.

LONDON: WEBBE, 3, BRYDGES STREET, STRAND.

## ONE PENNY WEEKLY.

# THE
# MYSTERIOUS MAN;
## OR
# THREE IN ONE.

**CATHERINE GRANTLY ATTEMPTS SUICIDE.**

## CHAPTER I.

### MORDENT GRANGE.

THIRTY years ago, near the village of Port Clinton, situated on the brow of one of the Blue Mountains, stood a large country mansion. It was known as Mordent Grange, and at the time we refer to, it was inhabited by Mr. Henry Mordent, a gentleman of large wealth, and his wife and child. The Grange was an irregularly built house of the Elizabethan style of architecture — and its quaint gables and gothic windows contrasted strangely with the more modern buildings in the village. The house was most beautifully situated, and the grounds were ornamented with all the elegance displayed by English noblemen around their country mansions. A handsome lawn, thickly studded with umbrageous trees, extended above the dwelling—while within a stone's throw the waters of the Schuylkill river could be seen sparkling through the foliage. A very fine garden, stocked with every kind of fruit tree, and another portion of it devoted to the culture of rare flowers, filled up the space behind the house to the precipitous mountain ascent.

From the elevated position of the Grange the view from it towards the south was most glorious—hill and dale, mountain and stream, white farm houses, and clusters of quiet villages, dark forests and green grass, grazing sheep and yellow corn, all formed a most magnificent panorama, which we do not believe could be surpassed.

Our story opens on a calm October night in the year 1830. The weather had been very warm during the day, but the evening was cool and pleasant. The sun a few hours before had tinged the west with her golden beams, and had sunk to rest in a blaze of glory. The hum of the busy world was silenced, and all nature seemed hushed to repose. Birds had ceased their flight and song, and save the murmuring of the breeze among the golden-leaved trees, and the gentle rippling of the Schuylkill, as it calmly flowed between its grassy banks, no sound reached the ear. The branches of the trees, as they waved to and fro, appeared to be whispering to each other mysterious secrets, and the mountains assumed vast and gigantic proportions in the dim twilight. The stars one by one peered out from the blue vault of heaven, and trembled with their own brilliancy. A little later, and faint streaks of silver light in the eastern horizon announced the coming of the queen of night, and in a few minutes she sailed with quiet majesty into the broad expanse of the heavens.

The moon's rays bathed the Grange in mellow light, and were reflected back by the old-fashioned gothic windows which faced the east. Had not the curtains of these windows been drawn close, they would have lighted up the apartment to which they belonged, and to which we must now conduct our readers. It was a handsomely furnished room, and a large blazing fire of wood which was burning on the hearth, added no little to its comfort. The walls were wainscoted and painted a light blue, curtains of the same colour hung in graceful folds from each window, and the carpet on the floor was of the most costly kind. Seated at a table, on which was placed a tea service, were a gentleman and lady; while a little boy about five years of age was playing in one corner of the room.

The gentlemen was Mr. Henry Mordent, and at the time we introduce him to the reader he appeared to be about forty-five years of age. He was handsome, intelligent, and happy. He used his large wealth to the best purposes, and was beloved by every one, as a noble, benevolent, and honourable gentleman. His wife, who presided at the tea table was many years younger than himself, and eminently beautiful in every acceptation of the word. Her complexion was as pure as the whitest alabaster, her hair a sunny auburn, her eyes heaven's own blue, and fringed with long curling eyelashes; her teeth were white and regular; her features cast in a classic mould, and her figure faultless. Her courtship had been a romantic one, and it is necessary we should hastily sketch it, that our readers may understand better what is to follow.

Catherine Grantly was the daughter of a wealthy farmer, living in Port Clinton. At an early age he had sent his daughter to a boarding-school in Harrisburg, where she received an excellent education, and returned home to her parents an accomplished young lady. It was at this time that Mr. Mordent made her acquaintance. He was immediately struck with her beauty, and visited her father's house every evening, although it was situated some three or four miles from the Grange. The great difference in their ages, doubtless, prevented him from proposing marriage so soon as he would otherwise have done. She had always treated him with kindness, and he even fancied that she sometimes entertained a warmer feeling for him. At last he determined that the next morning should decide his fate, and he rode down to her father's house at an earlier hour than usual. When he arrived there, he learned, to his horror, that Catherine had disappeared the night before, and nothing had been seen or heard of her.

A thousand surmises entered his mind to account for her absence At first he thought she might have eloped with some favoured suitor—but when he examined into her previous history, the idea was immediately scouted as untenable. About this time the neighbourhood around was ravaged by a band of robbers, headed by a notorious leader named Captain Rodolph. It was suggested by some one that the presence of these robbers had something to do with Miss Grantly's disappearance. Every possible effort was made to discover her whereabouts, but without success, and her poor father succumbed under the blow, and died of a broken heart. Mr. Mordent retired to his own home, and for weeks spoke to no one. By degrees, however, his intense grief became assuaged, and he entered the world again.

Six months after Catherine's disappearance Mr. Mordent was one day walking along the banks of the Schuylkill, when he saw a figure, clothed in white, rush towards the river, with her hair floating in the breeze. Arrived at the bank she tarried a moment, and then raising her hands to heaven dashed into the water, which immediately closed over her. To pull off his coat and watch, and to rush into the stream was for Mr. Mordent the work of a moment only. After a terrible struggle he succeeded in rescuing the young girl from a watery grave, and brought her to the shore. To his extreme surprise he found that the burden he bore in his arms was none other than Catherine Grantly.

He summoned assistance, and conveyed her to the Grange. The poor young girl who had just been saved from a watery grave was stricken down by a terrible fever. For long weeks she lay between life and death. At last youth and a strong constitution triumphed, and she was saved. During her illness Mr. Mordent watched her with the greatest care. Every day he would sit and watch by her bedside, and when she was able to listen he would read to her for hours together. Coming health restored beauty and grace to her features, which when she was rescued from drowning were wasted to a frightful degree by suffering of both a physical and mental character. Mr. Mordent every morning found his charming guest more beatiful and more lovely than ever; and he found in her conversation a thousand new charms—his passion returned with tenfold force.

Catherine's relatives had several times wished to remove her home, but Mr. Mordent had insisted that she should not leave his house until her health was completely restored. That time, however, was now rapidly approaching, and one fine summer afternoon Mr. Mordent told her how tenderly he loved her. When she heard the confession the young girl burst into tears, and heart-rending sobs wrung her bosom.

"O why did you save my life?" she cried, ringing her hands. "Why did you not let me die?"

The owner of Mordent Grange had never up to that time questioned her as to the motives which led her to commit suicide, But now he pressed her to reveal the truth to him. She related to him an account of all the trials and suffering she had undergone during her six months' absence.

It appeared that she had been seized while taking a walk, by a man on horseback; and after being gagged and blindfolded, she was conveyed away to some robber's resort in the mountains. She soon learned that her abductor was none other than Captain Rodolph, and that his motive for carrying her was to force her to marry him and share his crimes.

He appeared to take periodical visits to that neighbourhood, and when he did so he was the terror of the whole country round. A hundred plans had been set on foot to capture him, but they had every one failed. In one of his excursions he had chanced to see Catherine Grantly, and struck by her wonderful beauty he determined that he would obtain possession of her. Of course this could only be accomplished by force, and to force he resorted. When he made known his vile purpose to Cath-erine, she repulsed him with the utmost disgust.

Captain Rodolph, carried away by passion, and obeying the instincts of his brutal nature, had tried every possible means, and put into play every possible engine, to make her consent to his proposals—but she had the courage to resist everything. She braved prayers, tenderness, and threats. A knife which she had snatched from the robber's belt defended her from actual violence. Fearing that some snare would be laid to make her consent to his wishes, she refused all aliment, preferring death under the most hideous aspects to the shame that awaited her.

Her strength, however, soon began to fail her, and her mind to wander; she felt that the time would soon come when she could no longer struggle—when she was saved by the miraculous intervention of Providence.

Captain Rodolph, furious at his inability to overcome her resistance, suddenly changed his manner towards her. The love which he had felt for her was succeeded by the most intense hatred. He caused her to be confined in a species of dark and unhealthy prison, and appointed one of the most cruel and ferocious of his men as guard over her.

Catherine languished there two months, hoping every day that death would put an end to her sufferings. One day the jailor, struck no doubt by the hand of God, fell sick. In a short time the malady made rapid progress in his system, already broken down by every excess. Rodolph was absent with his men on some expedition far removed from the place where his prisoner was confined.

The robber left as guard, feeling that he was dying, and doubtless fearing to die alone, opened the door of the prison, and implored Catherine to render him good for evil, to nurse him in his last hours, and to forgive him for his conduct towards her. The unhappy girl, with a noble resolution, devoted herself to him who had tortured her, and who now implored her assistance.

Death approached; nothing could save the wretch. Touched by her generous conduct, the robber begged that she would immediately flee from the accursed place and leave him to his fate, at the same time informing her that it was Rodolph's determination to kill her when he returned, first, in revenge for the disdain with which she had treated him, and secondly, for the purpose of destroying all living proof of the crime he had committed. Catherine had it in her power to escape, but she would not leave the dying man.

At last death did its work, and the young girl was alone with the corpse. She was entirely ignorant of the situation of the place where she had been so long confined—and of course did not know which road to take. While debating in her own mind, she heard the footsteps of the robbers, who had returned, approaching the cell. She hesitated no longer—but opening a species of window which was level with the ground she left her hideous place of confinement. A thick wood was before her, and without knowing where she was going she rushed into the thickest of the bushes. She wandered about for many hours, and at last again came into the open country. She had scarcely done so, when, whether from terror or reality, she fancied she heard the sound of a horse's gallop in pursuit of her. Fear increased this sound into that made by Rodolph's whole band. She made a last effort, the river was close at hand, death was preferable to falling into their power, and she threw herself into the river, from which she was rescued, as we have already seen, by Mordent.

When she had finished her history, Mr. Mordent again begged her to listen to his suit. During the terrible recital of her suffering he had turned pale several times with indignation and anger; and made a vow that he would be revenged on the villain who had treated her so cruelly. His prayers and entreaties at length prevailed, and when her health was firmly established they were married. Six years of unbroken, unalloyed happiness had followed. One child had blessed their union, and on him both father and mother devoted the wealth of their love. And well did he repay their care and affection, for a more noble child could not be found, and even at his early age he had given proofs that he possessed a very superior mind. Having thus brought our readers to the time in which our story commences, we must return to the trio partaking of the evening meal in the parlour of Mordent Grange.

"I am very sorry, Henry," said Mrs. Mordent, "that Mr. Percival would not stay longer with us. Alfred was so fond of him."

"Percival is a strange fellow," replied Mr. Mordent, putting down his cup. "I would have used all my persuasive powers to make him stay, but I knew it would be of no use. When once he has made up his mind to anything, nothing in the world can ever change him."

"You have known him many years, have you not?"

"We were at the University together, and were great friends."

"He appears to be very fond of seclusion."

"He always was. He has strange tastes, and still stranger ideas. He dabbles with all the occult sciences, and pretends to have made some wonderful discoveries. He speaks French and German like a native, and is continually poring over German books."

"Father," interrupted the little boy, "I love Mr. Percival; he showed me such beautiful things in his room. When will he come back again?"

"He promised to visit us again in a few months, and he never breaks his word."

Their conversation was here interrupted by a tap at the door. And in answer to Mr. Mordent's summons of "come in!" the door opened, and a lad about eighteen years of age made his appearance. There was a look of consternation and fear depicted on his face.

"Why what is the matter, Bob?" said Mr. Mordent, good-humouredly. "You look as if you had seen a ghost."

Robert Bartol, or as he was more commonly call Bob, was a lad who had lived with Mr. Mordent since he was a child. From scullery boy he had risen to the important post of ostler. He was a good-hearted, good-tempered young fellow, and everybody was fond of him.

"Oh, sir!" said he—"I've heard dreadful news."

"What is it?"

"Why, Mr. Templeman's servant is here, and he says that his master's house was broken into last night, and everything valuable carried off."

"Is it possible?" said Mr. Mordent, a shade of uneasiness spreading over his face.

"Yes, sir—and they say—"

Bob hesitated.

"Say what?" said Mr. Mordent, in a sharp voice.

"They say, sir, that Captain Rodolph and his band are in the neighbourhood again."

Mrs. Mordent turned very pale when she heard this name mentioned.

"Nonsense!" said her husband, who had noticed her change of countenance. "There cannot be a burglary committed, or even a horse stolen, but it is immediately put down to the account of Captain Rodolph."

"But is it not more probable that it should be he than any one else?" asked Mrs. Mordent.

"No, my love; one would think that there was no other robber in the country than this Rodolph. Besides, I read to-day in the newspaper, that several atrocious robberies were committed a few days ago in York, and that the authorities had received positive information that they are the work of Rodolph and his companions. Now, as this wonderful robber has not the power of ubiquity, he cannot be in two places at the same time."

"I cannot overcome my dread of this man," said Mrs. Mordent. "I never hear his name mentioned but a cold shiver runs through my veins."

"My love, you must try and overcome this feeling—what have you to fear? Remember that six years have elapsed since that fearful time when you were in his power; besides am I not here to protect you?"

"I know, dear Henry, it is very foolish of me, but I never forget those fearful days of terror."

"Father," said little Alfred, running to Mr. Mordent, and turning up the sleeve of his dress—"I forgot to tell you that Mr. Percival said that he could take away this scar in my arm if I liked."

And he pointed to a deep white scar on his arm.

"The scar is not seen, my child, and with all due deference to Mr. Percival's skill, I think it had better not be tampered with."

The little child appeared to be perfectly satisfied with the answer, although he did not understand what it meant. He ran back to his corner again, and resumed his house building.

"Bob," said Mr. Mordent, "send Mr. Templeman's servant here, that I may question him about this robbery."

Bob left the room, and in a minute or two afterwards, Mr. Templeman's servant entered. Mr. Mordent interrogated him, but the information he received did not amount to much. No one had been seen to enter the house—and it was only in the morning that it was discovered that the dwelling had been entered during the night, and robbed of all its valuables.

The servant was dismissed with a gratuity; the tea things were removed; fresh hickory logs were thrown on the hearth, and shed a ruddy cheerful glow through the apartment. A little table was drawn up to the fire, and Mr. and Mrs. Mordent sat down to play a game at chess. The picture was one of domestic comfort, and under its influence Mrs. Mordent forgot all about Captain Rodolph, and the injuries she had experienced at his hands. Alfred soon grew sleepy, and his nurse was called, and after kissing his father and mother, and repeating his infant prayer at his mother's knees, he was taken to bed.

Mrs. Mordent was particularly fortunate that evening, winning three successive games. Her husband bore his loss with good humour, and at last the chessmen were put up, the table removed, and Mr. Mordent lit a cigar, and began to smoke. Mrs. Mordent went to one of the windows, and pulling the blinds on one side, she gazed on the scene without. The windows looked out into the garden. It was a glorious night—the moon was high in the heavens, and the shrubbery was bathed in its mellow light; the trees made long shadows on the gravelled paths, and the clear blue sky was studded here and there with some of the larger stars, shining like gems in the diadem of night. Suddenly Mrs. Mordent uttered a faint scream.

"What is the matter?" exclaimed Mr. Mordent.

"There is some one in the garden," said she, in a voice of alarm.

Her husband rushed to the window.

"Where?" said he.

"There—there!" said Mrs. Mordent, pointing to a cluster of shrubbery.

"I see no one, Kate."

"I distinctly saw a man's shadow on the path."

Mr. Mordent opened the window, and leaped into the garden. He ran to the spot indicated, and searched in every direction. In a few minutes he returned.

"Kate, your imagination has deceived you," said he. "I have searched the whole garden through and there is no one there."

"It is very strange," replied Mrs. Mordent—"I certainly thought I saw the shadow of a man clearly defined on the gravelled path. I even saw it move."

"It was most likely a gust of wind moving the branches of some of the trees."

"But there is no wind stirring to-night, Henry."

"The mention of that villain's name has excited you. Rely upon it, it was a delusion of your senses. But it is eleven o'clock," said Mr. Mordent, looking at his watch. "Let us retire, I have to be up early in the morning."

Mrs. Mordent lit her night lamp, and

they left the room together—but still there was an anxious expression on her face.

Soon afterwards lights the were extinguished one by one in the house—every sound was stilled, with the exception of the ticking of the old family clock on the stairs.

One hour after, however, had any of the inhabitants of that house been awake, they might have heard a low rasping sound, proceeding from the direction of the kitchen door. This was soon after followed by the creaking of hinges—and a sound of whispering might then have been heard in the hall.

----

## CHAPTER II.

### THE CAVERN IN THE MOUNTAIN.

FOR the proper elucidation of our story it will be necessary that we should go back a few hours in our history. About three miles from Mordent Grange, there was a deep defile in the very heart of the Blue Mountains, and it is to this spot that we have now to conduct our readers.

The sides of the two mountains forming this defile were precipitous and stony, and covered with that coarse stunted vegetation common to such soil. Tangled bushes, stunted fir-trees, and huge masses of rock, which rested on the brow of these eminences, and which appeared every moment ready to fall over, were to be met with in every direction, but still the scenery was very pituresque. Through this opening in the mountains, the white houses of Port Clinton, and the flashing Schuylskill could be seen meandering at the base of the neigh-bouring hill, while the trees peculiar to the region had assumed those gorgeous autumnal hues, which are the wonder and delight of all strangers.

About six o'clock in the evening on this same October day, a man might have been seen cautiously descending the precipitous descent to which we have just referred. A stranger observing him at a distance would have thought he was perilling his life, and expected to have seen him fall every moment into some of the deep chasms which appeared to be yawning for a victim. The sun was just setting in the west, and cast a glow of glory on the gorgeous vegetation around. One would have supposed that even the most uncultured person would have paused a moment to have observed the beauty of the scene, but this man turned neither to the right nor left, but proceeded steadily on his descent. Nor was his progress as dangerous as it had appeared at a

distance, for any one following his footsteps would have discovered rude steps which led down the mountain descent. An observer watching this man's progress would have seen him when about half-way down suddenly disappear. The said observer would then in all probability have supposed that his worst fears had been realized, and that the unfortunate man had precipitated into some of the chasms which abound on these mountains.

Such a supposition, however, would have been very far from the truth, for the man in question merely made a sudden turn round a huge mass of rock, which had rested perhaps for ages in the position it occupied. The situation of this mass was such, that it formed a narrow stone passage, which, however, at the distance of a few hundred feet, appeared to be entirely closed up by an impassable barrier of granite. As the person we have introduced to the reader is walking along the natural corridor, we will take the opportunity to give a slight description of him to the reader.

He was a man about thirty years of age, exceedingly strongly built, and his face was browned by the sun. His clothes were those of an ordinary countryman—and at first glance he might very well have passed for a farm labourer; but a more acute observer would have noticed two things incompatible with the supposition; the first was a long beard, not worn thirty years ago, and the other, that his hands showed no evidence of work. He walked with a measured gait, until he arrived at the very end of the passage. He then struck five blows on the hard stone before him—the first two slowly, and the other three rapidly. A moment elapsed, when a sudden tinkling of a bell could be heard, but so faint, that had he not been listening for it, it would in all probability have escaped his notice. No sooner, however, did he hear it, than he applied his lips to a small crevice in the solid piece of granite before him, and in a whisper pronounced the words, "*Three in One!*"

Immediately they were uttered, the solid rock rolled back on itself, and revealed a dark opening, not lofty enough for an ordinary sized person to enter, in an upright position.

The man bent his head and entered this opening. The moment he had done so, the rock rolled back again. A narrow passage, similar to the one he had just left, lay before him. It would have been entirely dark, had not lamps placed here and there lighted his steps. After proceeding along this passage a few yards, he came to a door, at which he knocked five times in the manner before described. Again was the same tinkling of the bell heard—this time, however, more loudly, but the man, instead of giving the same words as before, merely whispered the name "*Rodolph!*" The door opened, and he entered.

He found himself in a large natural cavern, which appeared to have been hewn out of the solid rock. It was very lofty, and lighted by a lamp which hung from the ceiling. The floor was covered with straw, and rude tables and benches were here and there placed about the apartment. In the solid walls of the cavern were two or three dark recesses which led into other compartments of the same cave. It was a gloomy, desolate place, and to a person entering it for the first time, an indescribable feeling of awe must take possession of him.

The cave was not unoccupied; at one of the tables three men were engaged playing dominoes, while another man lay seemingly fast asleep on a heap of straw in a corner. A little child, four or five years of age, was playing about as happy as if he had been in the open air, and two other children about the same age were slumbering in each others arms on a rude pallet.

"What the deuce makes you so particular, obliging me to go through all the forms before I could get in?" said the man as he entered.

"We only obeyed the captain's orders, Pete," said one of the men who was playing dominoes.

"It does seem to me such confounded nonsense," replied Pete. "You all knew I was out."

"We only obeyed the captain's orders," replied the man, again.

"All that I have got to say is, that it is confounded nonsense, the captain being so particular."

"What is that you say?" said the man lying on the straw, at the same time assuming a sitting posture.

"Nothing, captain, nothing," growled Pete. "I didn't know you were there."

Captain Rodolph is to play a very important part in our history, we must therefore intrude a slight description of him upon our readers. At the time of the commencement, he was about fifty years of age. He was very strongly built. His face was pale, and his features regular, and he might have been called a handsome man, had it not been for a ferocious-looking black beard, which covered his chin and upper lip. His hair was a dark brown, and his eyes, although small, were of that piercing character which shows cunning and subtlety. His bearing was decidedly military. He was tall in stature, but the most remarkable thing about him was the stern expression of his features, revealing indomitable will and determination. Any one skilled in physiognomy, the moment they saw his face, would immediately decide that he was a man who would scruple at nothing to accomplish his ends. He was dressed in homespun cloth of a gray colour; and round his waist was a belt in which was placed a pair of pistols, and a long knife in a sheath.

"Well, Pete, what news?" said Captain Rodolph, getting up on his feet.

"Nothing particular, captain."

"Does everything seem to be quiet?"

"Pretty quiet."

"Is there much talk about the affair at Templeman's last night?"

"Well, yes; there is a good deal of talk about it at the village."

"Are there any suspicions?"

"Nothing definite."

"Has my name been mentioned in connection with the affair?"

"Of course it has, captain. There never was a robbery committed in any part of the country in which your name has not been mixed up with it."

"True! but what matters; we are secure enough here."

Captain Rodolph was now silent, and leaning his elbow on the rude table, he appeared to be plunged into profound meditation. A silence fell over the inmates of the cavern, broken only by the click of the dominoes as they struck the table. Even the little boy made no noise. The captain suddenly rose on his feet.

"Andrew," said he, "come this way, I want to speak to you."

One of the men playing dominoes immediately rose up, and followed the captain into one of the dark entrances which we have before referred to. This natural doorway led into another apartment, about half the size of the one they had just quitted. It was lighted up in the same manner as the other, but there was a greater air of comfort about it. In various parts of this compartment of the cavern, were ranged weapons of almost every kind and description, guns, pistols, rifles, knives, were all mixed together.

Captain Rodolph sat down, and motioned for the man he had called Andrew, to follow his example.

"Andrew," said the captain, after a pause of some moments—"how long is it since I visited this part of the country?"

"It is six years, captain, since you were here."

"Yes, it is six years since," returned Rodolph, musingly—"well do I remember it. I am glad to find you have not forgotten it, Andrew."

"I shall never forget that time, captain, as long as I live."

"Let me see how well your memory serves you—for I have never mentioned the matter to any one since. What occurred during that time?"

"A woman escaped from the cave."

"True—her name?"

"Catherine Grantly."

"What effect had that escape on me?"

"You almost went mad with rage."

"Your recollection is excellent—what followed?"

"You took a solemn oath to be revenged."

"Have I kept that oath up to the present time?"

"Not that I am aware of."

"You are right, I have not. Fearful that our hiding place would be discovered, we immediately moved away. Six years have elapsed since that time, and we have returned here. It is evident that this girl could not tell the place where she was imprisoned, for our cave has not been visited during our absence. I sent you, Andrew, this morning, to make certain inquiries, and obtain certain information. Have you fulfilled my wishes?"

"I have."

"Tell me, then, what has become of Catherine Grantly?"

"She is married."

"Good! To whom?"

"Mr. Henry Mordent, of Mordent Grange."

"Mordent Grange—why, that is close by here."

"Three miles off—they were married almost immediately after her escape, and they have a little boy four years old."

"Indeed!" said Rodolph, in a musing tone. "What a strange coincidence!"

A silence of some minutes followed. Rodolph appeared to be revolving some plan in his own mind, or debating on some particular course of action. Suddenly he fixed a searching glance on Andrew's face."

"Andrew," said he, "can I trust you?"

"Well, captain," replied his companion, "you know best about that. I have now been a member of the band for twenty years, and during that time I have always done my duty."

"I know that, and it is because I have such confidence in you that I now speak to you. Andrew, six years ago I made an oath that I would be revenged on Catherine Grantly. You have just told me that you remember the circumstance perfectly well. Although so long a time has elapsed since I took that oath, I have not forgotten it. That time has now come to fulfil it."

Rodolph paused, and Andrew could see his eyes gleaming with the idea of vengeance. He even allowed himself to be so far carried away, as to convulsively grasp the handle of the knife he wore in his belt.

"What would you have me do, captain?" asked Andrew, when the pause had lasted more than a minute.

"Will you accompany me on an expedition to-night?"

"Certainly, to the end of the world, if you like."

"I knew I could trust you. You must promise me another thing, not to say a word of this to your comrades?"

"Have no fear on that score, captain, I will be as mum as the grave."

"Hold yourself in readiness to depart at ten."

"All right. Might I ask our destination?'

"Our destination is Mordent Grange."

"Have you anything further to say to me?" asked Andrew. "The rest of the band may think it strange that I am so long away."

"True—you had better now go and join your companions. I again caution you to be discreet, let not a word of our intended expedition escape your lips. On our way to the Grange I will enter more fully into my plans."

"You can trust me to the death, captain," said Andrew, rising from the seat, and re-entering the main compartment of the cavern.

"I thought you were never coming to finish your game," said his partner in the game of dominoes, which had been interrupted by Rodolph's summons. "What the deuce kept you so long?"

"The captain wanted me to clean a pair of pistols for him. But come, let's finish our game."

"I think the captain might have called' on somebody else who was not engaged, and have allowed us to finish our game," said the man, grumblingly.

Andrew made no reply, but sat down and resumed his game.

In the meantime, Captain Rodolph remained in the inner compartment of the cavern, with his elbows resting on his knees and his head resting on his hands. No one could read what his thoughts were, in that impenetrable face. His eyes were fixed on vacancy, and had it not been for an occasional knitting of the eyebrows, he might almost have been supposed to have been asleep.

Thus hour after hour passed away. At last the captain looked at his watch. It was exactly ten, and he abruptly rose from his seat, and entered the chief compartment of the cavern.

"A NIGHT OF HORRORS."

"Andrew," said he, looking about him for a minute, as if he were in doubt as to whom he should call upon, "come with me to make an examination of the neighbourhood. Pete, see that the sentinels are duly relieved; we may be gone two or three hours."

"Ay, ay, captain!" replied Pete; while Andrew jumped up and followed Rodolph out of the cavern. They passed along the stone passage until they came to the large rock, which appeared to prevent the further progress, but Captain Rodolph pressed

MYSTERIOUS MAN.—No. 2.

against it in a peculiar manner, and on one particular spot, and it revolved on itself. The moment they had passed out it assumed its natural position again.

In a few moments Rodolph and Andrew were standing on the brow of the mountain, with their faces bathed in the moonlight.

———

We must now transport our readers to the city. Exactly at the same hour that Captain Rodolph and Andrew quitted the cavern on their secret expedition, a gentleman was sitting alone in his residence in Broome Street.

The apartment he occupied was a species of study or library. It contained a large quantity of books, and an immense number of philosophical instruments of every description. The occupant was a man still young in years, although his thoughtful face and hair thickly studded with grey, gave him rather an elderly appearance. He was tall in stature, strongly built, and his features were regular, and had it not been for their sombre, thoughtful expression, he would have been considered exceedingly handsome. His age was not more than thirty.

This gentleman was Mr. George Percival, Mr. Henry Mordent's most particular friend. He had only lately returned from a visit to Mordent Grange. At the time we introduce him to the reader he appeared to be plunged in a profound reverie. He sat in a large easy chair, with his arms folded, and gazed intently on a mass of burning logs which were being consumed on the hearth. He was so much absorbed that he did not hear some one knock at his door, and it was only when the door opened and a gentleman appeared, that he was aroused from his reverie. The moment that he saw who his visitor was he rose from his chair, and extended his hand.

"I am delighted to see you, doctor," said Mr. Percival. "I said to myself to-day I wondered you had never called."

"I only heard this morning that you had returned from Mordent Grange, and I was determined not to let the day go by without seeing you, and this must plead my excuse for my late visit."

"Is it late?"

"Why, it's ten o'clock—but you are always in such a state of abstraction, that you never know how time passes. I knocked at the door two or three times, and you did not hear me."

"Indeed! I have to apologise—I know I am very absent."

"Still engaged in your old pursuits, I see!" said Doctor Burton (for such was the name of Mr. Percival's friend), glancing at the various philosophical and mathematical instruments lying about. Have you discovered the philosopher's stone yet?"

"Not exactly!" said Percival, smiling, "although in my opinion such a discovery is not an impossible one."

"I knew you would say that—how about the elixir vitæ?"

"You are only jesting with me, Burton, and I propose we change the subject. Now if you really ask me these questions from a desire to be instructed I should be very happy to give you my views—but I know

your practical nature too well not to be aware that you would not listen to me ten minutes."

"You are right, Percival—I really look upon you as a monomaniac, on the subject of the occult sciences. But answer me one question—what particular branch are you following now?"

"I am devoting my attention now to animal magnetism and the science of poisoning."

"The what?" exclaimed the doctor, in the utmost amazement.

"The science of poisoning!"

"Great heavens! what an awful study."

"You must not suppose I mean to put my discoveries to any bad use—I only pursue the study from the love of investigation."

"I am glad to hear you say that, for upon my word I began to look upon you as a second Cæsar Borgia!"

"Borgia—pshaw! he was but a novice in the art!" replied Percival, unlocking his drawer and taking from it a small covered box, which he opened. "Do you see the contents of that box?" he asked.

"Yes, I see a quantity of little glass globules."

"They appear harmless enough, do they not? and yet one of them dropped at your feet would kill you instantly."

"You are jesting."

"Not at all. To-morrow, if you will come to see me, we will try the experiment on some animal."

"But what do you propose to do with such awful things?"

"I have only made them as a matter of curiosity. One of them will kill an ox as suddenly as if it were struck with lightning."

"I will certainly visit you to-morrow—I should very much like to see the potency of these wonderful globules tested."

"Be here at ten o'clock in the morning. By-the-by, doctor, do you believe in presentiments of danger?"

"You know I am a practical man, Percival, and I must confess to you that I do not."

"Well, I do; the whole of this evening I've had an inexpressible feeling hanging over me, which I endeavour to shake off in vain. I am certain that I am about to hear bad news."

"Nonsense, you are dyspeptic and nervous—you don't take enough exercise in the open air."

"I know you physicians always argue in this way; but experience is worth all the theories in the world. I have never been deceived in these presentiments."

Doctor Burton argued the question for a

long time with his friend, but without being able to shake his faith. They then changed the subject, and after prolonging the conversation an hour, the doctor bade his friend good-night, and retired.

When he had gone Mr. Percival remained gazing on the fire for more than a quarter of an hour, he then rose from his seat and retired to his chamber. In a few minutes he was in bed. He was soon asleep, and for a short time his easy and regular breathing showed that his slumbers were calm and placid. But in a moment an extraordinary change took place; his breathing grew hurried, his face flushed, and he started up into a sitting posture, and gazed wildly around the room. When he discovered where he was he became calm again.

"My friend, Burton, would call this nightmare!" said he to himself.

Again he threw himself on his pillow and was soon fast asleep. But even in a less time than before the same thing took place again—and this time the impression appeared to be more vivid. Again he started up in his bed, and the perspiration rolled in large drops down his face.

"This is very strange!" he murmured, when he had recovered himself sufficiently to know that he was in his own chamber. But pshaw! it is but a dream!"

Once more he lay down. But his sleep was of even shorter duration than on the two previous occasions. This time his agony appeared to be intense, and with a single bound he jumped from the bed.

"I hear your shriek—it still rings in my ears!" he exclaimed, as he hurriedly dressed himself. "If possible I will save you."

So saying he rushed from the room.

## CHAPTER III.

### THE ROBBER'S VENGEANCE.

CAPTAIN Rodolph and Andrew after leaving the cavern, began slowly to descend the mountain. It was a glorious night; the moon sailed majestically overhead, and bathed every object in it silvery light. Not a single cloud was visible in the sky to veil the beauty of the stars, and the trees, clothed in their many-hued autumnal garments, acquired new beauties on that calm October night.

The robbers spoke but little on their way; Captain Rodolph in a few words detailed his plans, to which Andrew gave tacit consent. The latter appeared to be willing to follow his leader blindly in any-

thing that he might propose, and never dreamed for a moment of offering any suggestion of his own. In about an hour they stood before Mordent Grange. No light burned in the windows in the front of the house, and to all appearances every one had retired to bed.

"Andrew," said Captain Rodolph, "scale the garden wall, and see if there are any lights burning in any of the windows on this side of the house. Before we commence operations it is necessary that every one in the house should be asleep."

"All right, captain," replied Andrew, and with a single bound he leaped on the wall, and in another moment he had disappeared on the other side. In a very short time, however, he made his appearance again, and very precipitately rejoined his chief.

"There are persons still up in the apartment looking into the garden," said he.

"How do you know?"

"The room is lighted up, and I saw a lady at the window."

"Did she see you?"

"I am afraid she did, for I saw her move away with a gesture of alarm; for this reason I thought it better to leave the garden."

"You did right. We will crouch under this wall. They will in all probability search the garden. Should they search the outside, we can easily make our escape in the neighbouring thicket without being seen."

They both stooped down in the shadow of the wall, and almost holding their breath, listened attentively. In a few moments their expectations were realised, for they heard a man's step on the gravel walks. He was evidently searching the garden, for they could hear the shrubbery pushed on one side; then the sound of footsteps gradually subsided, and all was still again.

They waited nearly an hour, and then Rodolph sent Andrew again into the garden to explore. In a few minutes he returned.

"All quiet now, captain," said he.

"Are all the lights out?"

"Every one."

Captain Rodolph jumped over the wall, and stood beside Andrew in the garden.

"Have you examined the exterior of the house?"

"Yes."

"Where can an entrance be effected?"

"The kitchen door can be easily forced. I have brought my centre-bit with me."

"The kitchen door then let it be," returned Rodolph. And the two robbers, creeping as stealthily as cats, soon stood before the entrance they had determined to force. Andrew immediately fixed his centre-bit, and began cautiously to cut a piece out of the door a little above the lock. This was soon effected, and by inserting his finger he could push the bolt back. The lock was easily picked, and in a few moments they stood inside the house. With cautious steps they proceeded to the hall.

"Andrew, you unfasten the front hall door, while I go up stairs and execute what I have to do."

"All right, captain."

"You may then keep watch until you see me again : but be sure and have the entrance all clear, so that I can have a free exit."

"Everything shall be as you say, captain," said Andrew, and he proceeded to execute the commands of his chief, while the latter cautiously ascended the wide staircase.

When Rodolph reached the first landing, he paused a moment, and then lighting a dark lantern, he examined one by one the different doors opening on the corridor. At last he found the one of which he appeared to be in search. He stooped down and scrutinised the lock closely. This scrutiny appeared to satisfy him, for an expression of joy lighted up his face, and taking a pair of slender pincers, he inserted them into the keyhole, and in another moment the key which had been left in the lock on the inside was turned, and the door yielding to his efforts, he stepped into the chamber.

It was a handsomely furnished sleeping apartment which Captain Rodolph entered. A thick carpet covered the floor, mahogany chairs, and a centre-table to match, were arranged in different parts of the room, while a massive bedstead filled up a recess which appeared to have been specially made for that purpose.

This chamber was the sleeping apartment of Mr. and Mrs. Mordent. The former was fast asleep in bed, while the latter was asleep in a chair beside a child's crib, in which reposed her little boy. Not a sound save the calm and gentle breathing of the unconscious sleepers could be heard.

Rodolph drew his knife from his belt, and stealthily approached the bed; but in doing so, he caught his foot against one of the casters of the centre-table, and nearly stumbled. The noise he made immediately awoke the inmates of the chamber. Mrs. Mordent rose from her seat in the greatest alarm, and no sooner did she see who the intruder was, than she uttered a piercing shriek—

"Oh, God ! save us !—save us ! it is Captain Rodolph !" she exclaimed, in an agonized voice.

Before she had uttered these words, however, her husband had leaped from the bed, and had rushed to where the robber stood A terrible struggle ensued—but it was of short duration, for what could an unarmed man do against one who wielded a terrific weapon in his grasp? There was a scuffle —a few hurried exclamations, and then a heavy fall was heard. It was Mr. Mordent who had been struck to the heart by the cruel assassin. A smile of demoniacal triumph lighted up Rodolph's features, when he saw the result of his work. Mrs. Mordent appeared to be thunderstruck— her eyes were fixed—her face was as livid as that of a corpse, and her reason appeared to be dethroned.

"Catherine Mordent, hear me," exclaimed Rodolph. Six years ago you were in my power—you escaped from me. I then made an oath that I would be revenged. The hour for keeping my oath has come. There lies your husband—dead. Your life I shall spare, but your child shall be my next victim !"

So saying, he rushed to the crib, and before the distracted mother was even aware of what he intended to do, he had seized it in his arms, and rushed towards the door with it.

"Mother ! mother ! save me—save me !" cried the little boy.

The sound of her child's voice appeared to break the spell which had fallen on Mrs. Mordent.

"Monster !" she cried, "give me back my child. Take my life if you will, but spare my child."

And she rushed towards the assassin— but he had already left the room, and was descending the stairs. Maternal love appeared to give supernatural strength to the distracted mother, for by the time he had reached the hall she had caught up with him, and closing with him endeavoured to force her child from his grasp. In this she might even have been successful had not Andrew come to his chief's assistance. He held her back while Rodolph escaped by the hall door. He had not, however, proceeded many yards before Mrs. Mordent, by an extraordinary effort, freed herself from Andrew's grasp, and again started in pursuit of her son. By this time, however, Rodolph had begun to ascend the mountain.

"My child ! my child !" screamed the frantic mother.

"Ask for him in Satan's gulf, for that is his destination !" cried the robber, with a laugh of derision.

"O God ! you cannot—you dare not !"

"You shall see for yourself—come on !"

And the robber continued to ascend the mountain. Mrs Mordent followed, and evidently gained on him. When he had ascended about a hundred yards he made a sudden turn. The fact of his changing his course in this manner turned Mrs. Mordent's blood into ice, for she only knew too well where that path led. It was the only way of reaching a terrible abyss, known as Satan's Gulf. This abyss was a large opening in the side of the mountain, the depth of which had never been fathomed. The sides were almost perpendicular, and save a few stunted brambles which grew a few yards from the top, it presented, to the person who looked down into it, a black unfathomable pit. A rock thrown into this abyss was never heard to strike any bottom. It was towards this terrible precipice that Rodolph hurried. He reached it just as Mrs. Mordent caught up with him. When he stood on the edge of it he tossed the child in the air, and then with a cry of triumph he hurled it into the unfathomable abyss.

Mrs. Mordent stood for a moment rooted to the earth. All her faculties seemed to be paralysed. Her brain grew dizzy. She fancied she heard her child's voice appealing to her as it was descending that fearful gulf. She appeared to be influenced by a sudden resolution. She walked to the edge of the precipice.

"My child!" she exclaimed—"I come! I come!"

And with a shriek of agony and terror combined, she threw herself headlong into the terrfiic abyss.

## CHAPTER IV.

### A DOUBLE ALIBI.

EIGHTEEN years after the events detailed in the last chapter, on a cold, blustering March night, two pedestrians were slowly walking slowly in the city. It was about nine o'clock in the evening; in spite of the, comparatively speaking, early hour, owing to the inclemency of the weather, but few persons were in the street. The wind was particularly sharp and cutting, and whistled round the corner as if in very gladness at the discomfort it occasioned. The night was quite dark, not a single star could be seen, and the thick heavy clouds overhead presaged a coming storm. The two men to whom we have just referred were so earnestly engaged in conversation, that they did not appear to pay the slightest attention to the threatening weather.

The elder of the two was a man about fifty years of age; but he walked with a firm step, and appeared to be in the prime of life. His face was florid, his hair dark, without a single grey streak in it as yet, to denote he had commenced to descend the hill of life, and he was dressed in dark clothes, which admirably became his stout figure. His features, without being exactly regular, were decidedly handsome, and the expression was one of benevolence and good humour, united with firmness and strong determination.

His companion was much younger, evidently not being more than twenty-three years of age; and he was dressed with much more pretension, his clothes being of the newest cut and finest materials. At first glance he would be pronounced exceedingly handsome, but a more acute observer would pause before he gave an opinion as to his character, as revealed by the expression of his countenance. His forehead was lofty and intellectual; his eyes dark and piercing; on his upper lip he wore a small dark moustache, which to a great extent hid his mouth, but his lower lip was full and sensuous, and the absence of beard or whisker showed off his fine oval face to the best advantage. He was tall, strongly built, and had quite an aristocratic bearing.

We have already said that the pedestrians were walking slowly along; they continued to do so. The streets were nearly deserted, and it was not to be wondered at that the square into which they now turned was entirely so. Not a soul could be seen in any direction, and no sound save the howling of the wind through the leafless trees could be heard.

"You say this Captain Rodolph is in the city?" said the young man, to his companion, as they entered the square

"I have received the most positive assurance that such is the fact!" returned the other. "I have some police officers on his track, and I entertain strong hopes of being able to capture him. But he is no common robber, Mr. Mordent, and although he is steeped to his very eyes in crime, he adds to most remarkable bravery most extraordinary intelligence."

"I have heard marvellous stories about him—but I do not believe in them. You, Mr. Clair, as chief of police, know that the exploits of these kind of men are always exaggerated."

"I am fully aware such is the fact, but my official situation gives me an opportunity of knowing some of the actions of this villain. There can be no doubt but that the murder committed a few nights ago, near the river, was the work of his hands."

"Poor Captain Rodolph, I pity him!" said young Mordent, laughing, "there cannot be a single crime committed that is not blamed to him. One would suppose that he is the only criminal in the land."

"It seems to me, Mr. Mordent, that you are an apologist for this man, Rodolph ?"

"Not at all—but perhaps you accuse him wrongfully. How do you know that he committed the crime to which you refer ?"

"Two policemen recognised him."

"What ! did they see him ?"

"Yes !"

"Whilst he was committing the murder ?"

"No, but a few minutes afterwards."

"Where ?"

"In the street."

"And they did not arrest him ?"

"They tried—but he escaped."

"They knew him by description, then ?"

"Yes."

"Who gave them a description of him ?"

"I did."

"You ?" cried the young man, stopping suddenly, and gazing curiously into the face of the chief of police.

"Certainly !" replied his companion— "why should that astonish you ?"

"You have seen this robber, then ?"

"Yes, I have seen him."

"With your own eyes ?"

"With my own eyes."

"The deuce !" said the young man, biting his moustache, as if to prevent himself from laughing. "What sort of a looking man is he ? You can tell me, for I am your intimate friend ; besides, you may be serving the ends of justice, for you know I am about a good deal, and should I meet him I could have him arrested."

"I am perfectly willing to satisfy your curiosity, Mr. Mordent ; the description of this redoubtable robber is no secret. All the policemen in our large cities know it."

"Indeed ! well, let me hear it ?"

"Rodolph," began Mr. Clair, is a man apparently about your own age, and about your height and stoutness."

"The deuce he is !" replied the young man, in an angry tone.

"Do not be angry !" said the chief of police, smiling, 'the resemblance stops there."

"That's fortunate."

"His hair is black, and very long, hanging down on his shoulders. He always dresses in black, and wears a grey-coloured cloak. He generally rides a miserable-looking bay horse, with a white mane, to which, in spite of its sorry appearance, the most extraordinary qualities are ascribed."

"What a hideous-looking fellow he must be !" said the young man, with a gesture of disgust. "And are you really certain that this is the description of Captain Rodolph ?"

"Of course I am certain of it, I took it myself."

"But there is one thing in this that I cannot comprehend. This Captain Rodolph has been now before the people for more than twenty-five years. You know, Mr. Clair, that it was supposed that my father came to his death by his hands, although that was afterwards proved to be false. And that is eighteen years ago. Now the robber that you have described, you say is not apparently more than twenty-two or twenty-three years of age. How can you reconcile this discrepancy."

"Simply by informing you that he is so clever that he can assume almost any disguise he may choose. He appears to have the power of making himself look old or young at will. For many years nothing was heard of him—but latterly he has been as active as ever. Since he has been before the world there is no crime before the decalogue he has not committed."

"Let me ask you one more question ?" said the young man.

"Certainly."

"What was the date on which this horrible assassination near the river was committed ?"

"On the seventh of March."

"That is exactly six days ago."

"Yes."

"At what hour ?"

"About ten o'clock in the evening."

"You are certain of this ?"

"Quite so—the matter was thoroughly investigated."

"Very well, that is all I want to know."

"I have a call to make here for five minutes," said Mr. Clair. "If you will wait for me I will rejoin you, and we can walk down town together."

"All right, I will wait for you."

And the young man began to walk up and down the pavement humming an air, while Mr. Clair made his call. In a few minutes the latter re-appeared, and they then turned back again towards the city.

They continued to converse on various subjects, until they reached the Square. When they stood before the entrance of it, young Mordent seized his companion by the arm.

"Mr. Clair," said he, "if you have a few minutes at your disposal, I want you to pay a visit with me."

"Certainly !" replied the chief of police. "I am at your service. It would be very ill-natured of me, after dragging you out of your road, not go a little out of mine, for the sake of your company."

Instead of crossing the square, they turned into a street, and continued along it until they reached John-street. They proceeded down this dimly lighted thoroughfare for some distance, when Mordent suddenly stopped.

They stood before a house of mean appearance, the closed windows and doors of which either indicated that it was uninhabited, or that the inmates had all retired to rest.

" Which way now ?" said Mr. Clair.

" We stop here," replied his young friend. And then he added, " you say that it was on the night of the 7th of March that the murder was committed ?"

" Yes," said the chief of police, in a tone of surprise.

" And this crime you ascribe to Rodolph ?"

" Undoubtedly—but I am at a loss to know—"

" Why I repeat these questions? Have a little patience, and you shall know directly," interrupted his companion.

Young Mordent then approached the door and knocked loudly—there, however, was a peculiarity in the manner in which the act was performed which escaped the notice of the chief of police. After a few moments silence, a window situated in the second story was gently opened, and a man's head appeared at the casement.

" Who is there ?" cried a sonorous voice.

" It is I !" replied young Mordent.

" Who are you ?"

" What !" returned the young man, " is it possible you do not recognize me, Robert ?"

" Is that you, Mr. Mordent ?" returned the voice, with an accent of manifest satisfaction. " I beg your pardon for not recognizing you. " What can I do for you ?"

" Open your door, I want to speak to you."

Mordent had scarcely finished speaking, before the window was closed, and a moment or two afterwards the sound of heavy steps was heard. The front door was opened, and a man between forty and fifty years of age made his appearance on the threshold. He was dressed with that negligence which denotes the hurried toilet of a man awakened from his sleep.

" I am here, Mr. Mordent," said the new comer, " ready to do anything you may require of me."

" What does all this mean ?" said the chief of police, in a tone of voice clearly revealing impatience.

" It means, Mr. Clair," returned Mordent, " that I want to assist you in your enterprise."

" What enterprise ?"

" The capture of Captain Rodolph, which you are about to attempt to-night."

" Who told you that ?" said Mr. Clair, with a look of astonishment depicted on his face.

" No one ; but it was easy to be guessed. You think this man is in this city, and you have set every engine to work to arrest him. I have no doubt you have received some important information, and even your visit to the Square was on this business."

The chief of police appeared to reflect a few moments, he then said—

" I am free to confess, Mr. Mordent, that your skill at forming conclusions is remarkable. You have guessed right. I have received information, which leads me to expect, almost to a certainty, that Rodolph will be captured to-night."

" And it is for this very reason that I want to give you some important information, before you attempt to make the arrest you refer to."

" *You*, Mr. Mordent ?"

" I, myself, Mr. Clair."

" What is this information ?"

" You shall hear it from the lips of this man."

And Mordent pointed to Robert, who remained motionless on the threshold of his door, and appeared to wait for the young man's orders.

" Does this man know Rodolph ?" asked the chief of police.

" Yes," returned Mordent.

" He has seen him, perhaps ?"

" He has, a few days ago."

" Did he speak to him ?"

" He did."

" Then he can give me very important information."

" That is exactly what I thought."

" My dear Mr. Mordent," said the chief of police, shaking the young man by the hand with the utmost cordiality, " I can't thank you sufficiently for the favour you have done me by bringing me here. I will now interrogate this man."

" Excuse me," said Mordent, " if you question him, he will not reply. Let me speak to him, I know his manner."

" Do so," replied Mr. Clair. " I will leave everything to you."

Mordent advanced close to where the man called Robert stood. The above conversation had been carried on in a low voice, so that the latter had not heard a word of it.

" Robert," said young Mordent, in an imperative tone of voice, " you will reply without any hesitation to my questions ?"

" Yes, sir."

" How long have you been in this house ?"

" Four days."

" Where did you live before you came here ?"

" I lived near Harisburg."

" When did you leave there ?"

"Five days ago, that is to say, on the morning of the eighth ."

"What was your occupation?"

"I was a market-gardener."

"What was your reason for leaving your home ?"

"You know very well, sir, why I left."

"No matter—speak as if I did not know, and tell the reason to this gentleman who is with me."

"My story is a very simple one, sir," replied Robert. "I am fifty years of age to-day. For the first thirty years of my life I lived, as you are aware, on your father's estate, Mr. Mordent. He was a kind master to me, and may God bless his memory ! But you know what occurred, and I need only refer to it—a terrible crime was committed by some unknown hand. Your father and mother in one night were numbered with the dead. You were missing, and the estate was put into the hands of trustees. They were harsh men, and I was dismissed from employment. I left with my wife and children, and established myself as a market-gardner. I worked, and with the assistance of a kind Providence, I managed to pay my rent every year. But sickness invaded our dwelling—my wife was the first to succumb—my children followed. A violent hurricane, followed by a blight, utterly destroyed my garden, and I was a ruined man. My rent became due, and I could not pay it. The landlord seized everything I possessed in the world, and I was left penniless. Six days ago I was absolutely starving."

"That was the 7th of March, was it not ?" interrupted Mordent.

"Yes, sir," returned Robert, "I sat all day hungry and cold, and did not know where to look for a piece of bread. When night came, and I was about to throw myself on the floor in order to obtain a little sleep if possible—I suddenly heard the galloping of a horse outside my cottage."

"This was the night of the seventh, was it not ?" asked Mordent.

"Yes, sir, ten o'clock on the night of the seventh, I assure you. I shall never forget the day of the month to the last hour of my life. Suddenly I heard some one knock violently at the door. I thought at first that it was the sheriff's officer come to turn me out. I did not dare to open it, when the door yielded, and a man entered my apartment. This man had a strange appearance. His hair was black, very long, and hung down his shoulders. He was dressed in black, and he wore a grey coloured cloak."

"Dressed in black, with a grey-coloured cloak ?" cried Mr. Clair, in a voice of surprise.

"Yes, sir, and he had also a long black beard, and dark, piercing eyes."

"Impossible !" interrupted the chief of police—"but go on."

"The stranger advanced and threw at my feet a purse. 'There is £500,' said he. 'It is no use your staying here. Go tomorrow to this address.' He then put into my hands a little piece of paper. Having done this, he turned round and left the house, and mounting his horse again, rode away."

"Did you notice the horse ?" asked the chief of police.

"Yes, sir, I did, for the horse was a very remarkable one. It was a bay with a white mane, and such a wretched looking animal, that it appeared impossible that it could sustain the rider's weight ; but no sooner had he leaped on its back than it neighed, and seemed animated by a strange ardour. Stupefied, and half-crazy with joy, I followed this singular personage. Just as he was about to start off, I rushed towards him. 'What is your name,' I asked, 'that I may treasure it up in my heart ?' 'My name is an accursed one,' he replied. 'I am Captain Rodolph !' And so saying, he started off at an extraordinary pace—the horse did not appear to be the same one that I had seen."

"What followed ?" asked Mordent, noticing that the chief of police was plunged in a profound reverie.

"The next day, sir, I started for the city, and came to this house—for that was the address given me on the piece of paper. When I came here, I found a man in possession, who gave me the key without uttering a word, and then left me. Since that time, that is to say for five days, not a living soul has been here, excepting you, Mr. Mordent, to whom I related this history."

Mordent turned towards the chief of police. The latter appeared to be absorbed in a world of reflection ; he made an effort, however, to chase away the clouds which obscured his mind, and addressing Robert, exclaimed—

"You alone saw this man ?"

"No, sir, three other persons saw him, and can testify to the truth of my story."

"Who are they ?"

"The first is a policeman, who saw him ride through the streets, and who mentioned the fact to me the next day. The other two were a farmer and his son, living in the neighbourhood, who were driving a load of hay to market, and saw him ride along the road."

"You say it was ten o'clock on the night of the 7th of March that this man called at your house ?" asked the chief of the police.

CAPTAIN RODOLPH IS VERY NEARLY CAUGHT.

" It was about ten o'clock on the evening of the 7th, sir.

" And at what hour was the murder committed near the river?" asked Mordent, addressing Mr. Clair.

" About ten o'clock on the evening of the 7th," replied the latter.

Young Mordent turned towards the man they had been interrogating.

" Thank you, Robert," said he, " you can now go in. I have nothing more to ask of you. Good night !"

Robert bowed, and entering the house

again, closed the door, while the chief of police and his companion began slowly to retrace their steps.

" Well, Mr. Clair," said Mordent, " how can you reconcile the fact that on the same night the same man, at the same hour, seen by four different witnesses in the neighbourhood of Harisburg, a hundred miles from here, could have committed the murder near the river."

" How long have you known this man Robert ?" asked the chief of police, instead of replying to the question addressed to him.

"He told you himself just now. He was born on my father's estate, and knew me from a child."

"I remember now," said Mr. Clair, "he was one of your principal witnesses, when you brought the suit to obtain possession of your patrimony, of which you had been so long deprived, owing to the fact of your having been carried away when a child?"

"Exactly so. Robert loved my father. He remembers the circumstance of my birth perfectly well. I used to play with him when a child. And on that fatal night when my father was killed, and my mother mysteriously disappeared, he saw me carried off by the assassin who murdered my father. If you remember, when the court heard his testimony, they at once gave a verdict in my favour."

"I remember the circumstances perfectly well now."

"I may add, that I know Robert to be a man of unimpeachable veracity."

"I have no doubt of the truth of his story," replied Mr. Clair.

"Well, what do you think of the whole affair?"

"I think, Mr. Mordent, that it is a much more extraordinary and mysterious affair than I at first supposed."

"After making these remarks, Mr. Clair seemed to be plunged into an ocean of reflections. Young Mordent walked side by side with him, and respected his silence. He hummed an air from the last opera, and appeared from his careless demeanour to have forgotten all about the subject they had been discussing. While they were proceeding in this manner leisurely down the street, a policeman approached.

"A despatch for you, Mr. Clair," said he, touching his hat, and handing to the chief a large envelope sealed. "I judged it was of importance, so I thought I would meet you with it, as I knew which way you would come."

"You did right, Baxter," returned Mr. Clair, going under a gas lamp and breaking the seal.

Suddenly he uttered an exclamation of surprise, as he eagerly read the contents of the letter.

"What is the matter?" asked Mordent, with much curiosity.

"It is absolutely incredible!" replied the chief of police.

"Might I venture to ask the contents of that communication?" said Mordent.

Mr. Clair made a sign to the policeman that he might go back, and the latter obeying, they were alone again.

"The despatch I have received concerns this Rodolph," said he, "and really when I read it, I almost fancy I am dreaming."

"What in the world do you mean?"

"I am going to treat you confidentially."

"You may rely upon it that I will not abuse your confidence."

"Well, then, it appears that this Rodolph has a number of bands of organised robbers in different parts of the country. We hear of them everywhere."

"Why, this captain appears to command a whole army—he certainly ought to receive the title of general."

"It is not a question to jest about. This organization of robbers is a formidable one. Now this despatch comes from the chief of the police, and informs me that a band of robbers commanded by Captain Rodolph in person, made an attack on a farm-house on the 7th of March, and pillaged it from top to bottom."

"What!" cried Mr. Mordent, "is it possible on this same 7th of March?"

"Yes, he was seen by numerous persons—and in the despatch, his appearance is exactly described as we have heard it—even down to his extraordinary looking horse. What do you think of it, Mr. Mordent?"

"I think that this robber is endowed with ubiquity, and can be in half a dozen places at the same time."

"I see you treat the matter as a jest, but I must confess that I am fairly puzzled."

By this time they had reached the central police station, and Mordent stopped and looked at his watch.

"I suppose you are going to attend to your business, Mr. Clair," said he; "but before you go, will you allow me to ask you a question or two?"

"Certainly, I shall be glad to give you any information I can."

"If I understand right, you intended to put into play to-night every engine in your power, for the purpose of arresting this Captain Rodolph?"

"That is perfectly true."

"Is that your intention, now?"

"Yes, it is my intention now more than ever."

"Even after what you have heard from Robert, and from the head of the police in Richmond?"

"Undoubtedly; there is a mystery in this affair which it is my duty to clear up, if possible."

"Are you certain that Captain Rodolph is now in this city?"

"I am certain of it."

"And nothing can make you change your resolution?"

"Nothing! but allow me to say to you in my turn, that I cannot understand the interest you appear to take in this robber."

"Mordent bit his moustache with manifest impatience. He appeared to be debating something in his own mind. At last, after a pause of a few moments, he spoke—

"The interest I feel in this robber is easily explained, Mr. Clair, when you remember what passed during the trial by which I was reinstated in my property. You recollect that for fifteen years I was in the power of a wretch, and it was supposed that it was Captain Rodolph who thus illegally robbed me of my liberty. It was also stated that it was he who murdered my father. But on the trial all this was proved to be false. I therefore consider that I owe some recompense to the man, who, at least as regards myself and my parents, has been fearfully maligned. It may be a weakness on my part, and doubtless appears very strange to you ; but to me he is an innocent man, accused of a crime he never committed, and who knows if this false accusation may not have caused him to take a bad course of life ?"

The chief made no reply, but he appeared to be struck by what the young man had said.

"But I wish to speak to you on another subject," added Mordent, lowering his voice, and speaking almost in a caressing tone. "You are doubtless aware why I frequent your house so much ? The beauty of your charming daughter, the precious qualities of her heart and mind, have lighted up a passion in my heart which I have sometimes fancied you have approved."

"A marriage, Mr. Mordent, between our families is honourable for both of us," interrupted Mr. Clair.

Mordent bowed, while a smile of gratification and triumph lighted up his features

"Deprival of your parents, Mr. Mordent," continued the chief of police, "alone as you are in the world, I shall be happy to be drawn in close bonds of relation to you, and am quite willing to confide my dear daughter Ellen to your care. I would be a father to her and to you."

"If you consider me almost in the light of a son, and if I regard you from the present moment as a father, you can understand that my advice is that of a devoted friend. Take my advice, and have nothing to do with this affair of Captain Rodolph. I am certain that this man is innocent of the crimes you impute to him, as he was of that he was accused in regard to myself. Have nothing to do in anything that concerns him."

"Why ?" asked the chief of police.

"Because you will only bring misfortune on yourself."

"Do you really think so ?"

"I am certain of it."

"But how can you know that ?"

"I know—I have a presentiment that such will be the result—and this presentiment never deceives me—although I cannot explain it to another party."

"That is no reply to my question," said Mr. Clair, smiling.

"My dear sir, be satisfied with it, and take my advice."

"Mr. Mordent," said the chief of police, in a grave voice, "I have certain duties which my oath of office compels me to perform. Give me good reasons for your opinion, and then, perhaps, I might listen to your advice."

"I cannot give you any other reasons than those I have already mentioned."

"Then, my dear young friend, you must not be surprised that I do my duty."

Mordent made an impatient gesture.

"You are really decided ?" said he.

"Perfectly so !"

"Well, luck attend you! Good-bye, till we meet again."

"Good-bye !"

The young man shook hands with Mr. Clair, and then hurried away. The chief of police followed him with his eye until he was out of sight. He then entered the station house, but his forehead was clouded as if some important matter weighed heavily on his mind.

——

## CHAPTER V.

### THE THREE SPIES.

MR. CLAIR retired to his own private room, and ordered Baxter, the man who had brought him the despatch to be sent to him.

James Baxter, a lieutenant in the police force, was a man about forty years of age. His face, to an ordinary observer, would have been called a fine open countenance, but a more acute physiognomist would have been able to trace something deceitful in his restless eyes, and in the expression of his mouth. When he entered the chief of police's presence, the latter was so deeply absorbed by his own thoughts that for a few moments his visitor stood there without being recognized. At last Mr. Clair looked up.

"Ah, Baxter !" said he, "you are here, I see ?"

"I believe you sent for me, sir ?"

"I did—Baxter, I believe you have been about fifteen years in the service of the police, have you not ?"

"Fifteen years and seven months."

"You have been a good officer."

"I have done my best, sir."

"I believe you have looked upon me as your friend."

Baxter bowed his acknowledgment.

"What should you say if I made you a present of five pounds from my own private purse?"

"I should say," replied Baxter, "that you were very liberal, but that it was unnecessary to reward me for doing my duty."

"Well, Baxter, you can make this money to-night, and at the same time show your zeal for the service."

Baxter drew himself up to his full height, and was all attention.

"Listen to me!" said Mr. Clair, after a moment's pause, "the house, No. 209, John Street, is a miserable-looking dwelling, and stands by itself. Do you know it?"

"Yes, sir, I have remarked it frequently in my rounds."

"Well, that house is occupied at present by a man about fifty years of age, who goes by the name of Robert. I want to know more about him."

"You wish me to arrest him?"

"No, but simply put on plain clothes and watch the house—do not let the least thing, however minute, escape your notice."

"I understand, sir."

"I give you full power in this delicate business. Employ whom you will — do whatever you think best—but let nothing escape you."

"You may rely upon me!" said Baxter.

"Go and make the necessary preparations—but come here again before you start."

Baxter left the room, and Mr. Clair, leaning his elbow on the table, and resting his head on his hand, again gave himself up to his own reflections.

"I am determined to possess the key to these mysteries." thought he. "This night I will have this villain, Rodolph, arrested, and then I will have him confronted with this man who pretends to have seen him, and whose strange story demands the most minute investigation."

Baxter at this moment entered.

"Have you any further instructions to give me?" said he.

"No!" returned Mr. Clair. "I only ask you to be prudent, active, and discreet."

"You may depend upon me, sir."

So saying, he again left the chief's private office, and having dressed himself in citizen's clothes, he started off. As he walked along, he muttered to himself—

"Five pounds is a very nice present—but Captain Rodolph is a better friend, and much more generous than the chief of police."

After Baxter had left the room, as Mr.

Clair supposed to perform the task that had been assigned to him, the former sat down at his desk, and was soon deeply engaged in writing. He had not, however, written more than a page or two, when a messenger came to inform him that the mayor of the city wished to speak to him. Mr. Clair ordered the mayor to be immediately admitted.

"Well, Mr. Clair," said the chief magistrate, as he sat down, "what is the news?"

"Excellent news, Mr. Mayor."

"You refer to this villain, Captain Rodolph?"

"Yes."

"Do you think you will be able to capture him this time I am perfectly certain of it."

"You have all your men on the alert?"

"Every one of them."

"But do you think it probable," said the mayor, "that Rodolph wears his ordinary dress by which he is known."

"I think it hardly probable—he is most likely disguised."

"What is the disguise he has assumed?"

"Of that I am entirely ignorant—but I hope in a quarter of an hour to be able to satisfy you on that point, Mr. Mayor."

"How is that?"

"I have other spies in the city."

"Indeed! who are they?"

"Three men who once belonged to Rodolph's band, who for five hundred dollars have consented to deliver up their chief to us to-night."

"I trust you may be successful, Mr. Clair, said the mayor, "and that we shall be able to find a solution for the mysteries connected with this extraordinary man."

"In ten minutes, Mr. Mayor, my three spies will be here to make their report."

"I will wait to hear the result," said the mayor.

Mr. Clair went on with his writing, and the mayor took up a paper to read, but in less than ten minutes the sound of footsteps was heard in the passage, and in a moment or two afterwards a knock was heard at the door.

"Come in," cried Mr. Clair, and then turning to the mayor, he added—"here is one of my spies."

"Now we shall know the truth," said the chief magistrate of the city, rising from his chair.

"The door turned on its hinges, and a man entered. He was clothed in rags, his face had that low and repulsive expression which reveals a scoundrel of the very lowest class. As he entered the chamber he made a low bow.

"Come nearer, rascal!" said the mayor, without even attempting to conceal the disgust the presence of this miserable wretch inspired him with.

"I am at your orders, Mr. Mayor!" said he, bowing still lower.

"Ah! you know me, then!" said the chief magistrate.

"Who is there that does not know the mayor?" cried the spy, with bold effrontery.

"Well, all that I have to say to you is," said the chief magistrate, "that if you have failed in what you undertook, you must expect no pity."

"And if I have succeeded?"

"I will ratify the promises made to you by the chief of police."

"That is to say, one hundred pounds in my pocket, and a free pardon?"

"Yes!" returned the mayor.

"Then you may begin to count out the money!" said the spy, addressing Mr. Clair.

"You have succeeded then?" said the latter.

"Yes, sir."

"You can deliver Captain Rodolph up into our hands?"

"Yes, sir."

"To-night?"

"In five minutes."

The chief of police cast a look of triumph at the mayor.

"Where can he be found?"

"Captain Rodolph is at this moment in at Delmonico's, eating oysters."

"How can he be recognized?"

"He is dressed as a countryman, in homespun cloth, and a large white beaver hat, and he carries a large whip in his hand."

"Come along with me, my man!" said the chief of police. "I will go and arrest him at once."

So saying, he advanced rapidly towards the door—but he had no sooner reached the threshold, than the door was burst violently open, and a second personage, better clad, and not nearly as repulsive looking as the first spy entered. As soon as he saw the mayor, he made a low bow, but before they could interrogate him he spoke.

"Mr. Clair," said he, "if you want to take Captain Rodolph, there is not a moment to lose."

"You have seen him then?" asked the chief of police.

"I have just spoken to him."

"He is in Delmonico's, is he not?"

"Delmonico's!" cried the second spy, in astonishment. "You are wrong, sir! Captain Rodolph is at this moment in the bar-room of the St. Nicholas Hotel."

"Rodolph in the St. Nicholas Hotel?" said the chief of police; "but did you not tell me just now," he added, turning to the spy, "that he was in Delmonico's?"

"Certainly, and I maintain what I said is true," returned the party addressed.

"How was he dressed?" asked the chief of police, addressing the second spy.

"He was dressed in military costume, and any one would take him for a member of the 7th regiment."

"It is very certain one of you has deceived me—woe be to him who has done so!"

"Does that man pretend to have seen the captain?" said the new comer, regarding the first spy with a look of supreme disdain.

"Yes, and I affirm it again," replied the latter, "and I tell you, Bexley Jem, you lie in your teeth, if you maintain the contrary."

Jem, as he was called, strode up to the first spy, who went by the euphonious name of Welling Redneck.

"Do you dare to maintain," said the former, with an angry tone and gesticulation, "that you saw Captain Rodolph anywhere else excepting in the bar-room of the St. Nicholas Hotel?"

"Yes, I contend that I saw him in Delmonico's, and that he was disguised as a countryman."

"And I maintain that I saw him in the St. Nicholas Hotel, disguised as a soldier."

The mayor and the chief of police were silent and embarrassed in the face of these statements, so diametrically opposed to each other, and yet maintained with so much energy.

"What o'clock was it when you saw him?" asked the chief of police, addressing Redneck.

"It was exactly nine o'clock by the City Hall clock, when he entered Delmonico's," replied the man.

"Why, it was exactly nine o'clock by the timepiece of the St. Nicholas Hotel barroom, when I spoke to him there," said Bexley Jem.

"How, in the name of all that is wonderful, could he be in two places at the same hour dressed entirely different?" said the chief of police. "One of you has evidently deceived me."

"I will take an oath that what I say is the truth," said Redneck.

"I swear that I do not lie about the matter," said Jem."

"Mr. Clair," said the first spy, "I know Captain Rodolph perfectly well. I was a member of his band for six months," said Redneck.

"And I was with him for more than a year," said Jem.

"I spoke to him with my own lips."

"I saw him with my own eyes. Let the chief of police accompany me to the St. Nicholas Hotel, and I will engage to deliver Captain Rodolph into his hands."

"If Mr. Clair will give orders for some one to accompany me, and if he does not find Captain Rodolph at Delmonico's, I am perfectly willing to be sent so prison for life."

At that moment a knock was heard at the door.

"Ah, here is Lester—we shall now know the truth!" said the chief of police. And he ran to the door and opened it, admitting the third spy, who, although better dressed than the two others, did not appear to be much better off in a moral point of view. The chief took him by the arm, and drew him into the middle of the chamber with an energy which revealed the perplexity into which he was plunged.

"Have you seen Captain Rodolph?" he asked, in an abrupt tone of voice.

"I have!" replied Lester.

"At what o'clock?"

"Just as the clock was striking nine—that is to say, about ten minutes ago."

"Good!" said the chief, with a deep breath of satisfaction, "and where did you see him?"

"I saw him enter a house in Bond Street."

"In Bond Street!" cried Mr. Clair; he, the mayor, and the other two spies regarding Lester with an air of perfect stupefaction.

"Yes, sir," replied Lester, quietly, "I saw him enter No. 211, Bond Street, exactly as the clock struck nine."

"Impossible!" said the chief.

"I assure you, sir, I tell the truth; he was dressed in black, and wore a gray cloak."

"Impossible!" cried the mayor.

"I know the captain as well as I do my own brother!" said Lester, with an air of confidence. "Not only did I see him but I spoke to him, and he ordered me to keep an eye on the chief of police."

"If I arrest everyone in the City to-night," said the chief of police, stamping with his foot on the floor, "I am determined that I will have this man."

And he immediately ordered three separate squads of policemen to go to all the places where it was stated that Rodolph had been seen; he himself accompanying one of the parties.

———

## CHAPTER VI.

### THE SHADOW ON THE FLOOR.

WE must now conduct our readers to the interior of a handsome dwelling, situated in Bond Street. The time is about an hour after the events re-

lated in the last chapter. The interior of the house is handsomely furnished, and reveals that the tenant is in easy circumstances. This house is the residence of Mr. Clair, chief of police.

In the front parlour of this dwelling, at the house we refer to, a bright fire was burning; a thousand sparks from the dry logs leaping up the broad chimney with a cracking sound, which, on a chilly, blustering March night makes most excellent music. Seated at a table, placed in the middle of the room, were two young girls, both of them so beautiful, so graceful and so exquisitely formed, that it would have puzzled the greatest connoisseur of female beauty to decide between them. And yet they were essentially different.

The one seated nearest the fire was a brunette. Her magnificent hair, black as a raven's wing, and extremely thick and abundant, was twisted carelessly around her beautifully shaped head, and fell in voluptuous negligence on her alabaster shoulders. Her large black eyes had that dreamy expression given to them by the long eyelashes and beautifully pencilled eyebrow. Her complexion was clear, and the hue of perfect health tinged her cheek. She was rather tall in stature, but her form was faultless, the tight-fitting dress she wore set off the admirable contour of her figure to the greatest advantage. Her features were of Grecian regularity, and every time she smiled she revealed two rows of pearly teeth, as white and regular as if they had been cut from the solid ivory. If any fault could be found, it would be in the extreme smallness of her hands and feet.

This young lady was Ellen Clair, daughter of the chief of police, and now in the eighteenth year of her age.

Her companion was about a year younger than herself, and was just as fair as the other was dark. Her hair was a sunny auburn, her eyes a heavenly blue, her complexion as fair as a lily, and her figure as graceful as that any sculptor could fashion. Her name was Ada Meredith, and she was Miss Clair's bosom friend. At the time we introduce them to the reader they were both employed in fancy work; at the same time being engaged in confidential conversation.

"I must confess, dear Nelly," said Ada, in reply to some remark made by her friend, "that I do not exactly understand your objection to Mr. Mordent. You must agree that he is handsome?"

"O, yes, he is handsome enough!" replied Ellen.

"He is polite, agreeable, and his manners are good."

"That is true—but still there is something about him I do not like. I have a decided antipathy to him."

"How strange—but perhaps, darling, your affections are already engaged?"

"No, I assure you such is not the case. I have not yet seen the man I would like to marry."

"Mr. Mordent has never proposed to you?"

"Never, but his attentions cannot be mistaken. He visits here as you are aware, almost every evening, and pays me a thousand little attentions which speak more than words. I wish, dear Ada, since you are such an admirer of him, that you would set you cap for him, as the saying is."

"What chance should I stand against you, Nelly? Besides, I know nothing at all about him. By-the-bye, your father seems to like him very much."

"Yes, and it gives me a good deal of uneasiness. I am so afraid father will ask me to marry him. If I tell him I do not love Mr. Mordent, he will require some reason, and upon my word I do not know what to say."

"Oh, never fear—your father, I am sure, will never force you."

Their conversation was here interrupted by the entrance of Mr. Clair. He appeared fatigued and careworn, and threw himself into his easy chair, without uttering a word. Ellen rose from her seat, and approaching her father, kissed him.

"You appear to be very tired to-night, father!" said she.

"Yes, my child, I am very much fatigued both in body and mind."

"Your duties are too arduous—why do you not resign your appointment?"

"You don't understand this matter, Nelly. My honour forbids me to resign at the present time."

"Why, father, you promised me that you would resign as soon as this Captain Rodolph was captured."

"So I will."

"But I thought you were certain that he would be arrested to-night?"

"So I expected, for I had received the most positive information as to his whereabouts, and three of his band promised to place him in my hands—but I have failed. But we will dismiss the subject, for I have been made the victim of so much mysticism to-night, that I cannot bear to think about it. By-the-bye, Miss Meredith," added Mr. Clair, addressing Ellen's companion, "have you heard anything lately of your friend, Mr. Percival?"

"Nothing directly!" replied Ada; Dr. Burton informed me the other day that he is still in the western prairies; and he has no idea when he will return. You know he is very eccentric in his movements, that he can never be counted on."

"I wish to heaven he was here; I should like to have his counsel and advice. He possesses such a clear head, that he would be of the greatest use to me just now."

Mr. Clair grew silent and thoughtful. Ellen presented him with a cigar and a light, and under the influence of the sedative weed the anxious expression of his face vanished, and he became entirely himself again.

"Dear father!" said Ellen, after the pause in the conversation had lasted some minutes, "I want you to satisfy my curiosity on one point—and that is, what kind of a looking man is this Captain Rodolph?"

"I see he is a hero in your eyes!" replied Mr. Clair, laughing. "Well, my child, he is quite handsome, and strange to say, bears quite a resemblance to Mr. Mordent. His features are regular, he is tall in stature, and wears a heavy black beard."

"How is he generally dressed?"

"Well, he assumes a great number of disguises—but his ordinary dress is black, and in winter he wears a gray-coloured cloak. But there are other mysteries about him, which, for the life of me I cannot understand, and one of them, strange as it may appear in your ears is, that he appears to possess the power of ubiquity."

"You are jesting, father."

"Of course, I know it is impossible, and yet I have received the strongest evidence that such is the fact this very night. It has been reported to me by numerous witnesses that he was seen at nine o'clock in three different places, and in different dresses."

"Of course, there is some mistake about it?"

"I suppose so—but I assure you, Nelly, I am utterly at a loss to explain it."

A servant now entered the room, and informed Miss Meredith that her father's coachman had come to take her home. Hastily putting on her things, and bidding her friend an affectionate good-night, Ada left the house.

"Come, my child!" said Mr. Clair, rising from his chair, "it is time we were in bed!" and kissing his daughter, he was about to leave the room, when a sudden idea appeared to strike him.

"Nelly," said he, with a meaning smile, "has Mr. Mordent been here to-night?"

"No, not to-night, father!"

"I have something particular to say to you concerning him—but I will defer it until to-morrow."

They then retired to their respective chambers.

When Ellen Clair entered her bedroom,

she threw herself on a chair, and began to reflect on her father's last words. She felt certain that it had reference to an offer of marriage from Mr. Mordent; she then interrogated her own feelings with respect to her suitor, and found that from some cause which she could not account for herself, she positively disliked him, and determined that she would be firm to her father. She then commenced her toilet for the night, first of all letting down her abundant hair, and going to the glass she began to brush it. While she was thus occupied she gave a slight start, for reflected in the mirror she saw the shadow of a man's hand on the floor. Ellen Clair was a brave girl, and recovered herself in an instant, and went on brushing her hair as if she had seen nothing. It is true her heart beat faster than usual, but she revealed by no outward sign her knowledge of anyone being in the room. She calmly and deliberately began to examine, by the aid of her looking glass, the position of the intruder. She soon found that he was concealed under an old-fashioned bureau. All this time she went calmly on, adjusting her hair, and when she had finished this part of her toilet she moved about the chamber with as much ease as if she had been alone. During all this time she was revolving in her own mind the best course for her to pursue. She had locked her door on entering, and she knew that if she were to attempt suddenly to escape, before she could unlock the door, the robber would be able to stop her progress. While she was thus debating she walked cautiously round the bureau, and on the other side of it she saw protruding a portion of a *gray cloak*.

"It is Captain Rodolph!" she murmured to herself, and then sat down for the purpose of collecting her thoughts.

---

## CHAPTER VII.

### THE MAN WITH THE GRAY CLOAK.

LET us now return to young Mordent, who the reader will remember left the chief of police just before the latter entered his own private office. He walked some distance down the street, and then suddenly turned round again and took the same course he had followed with Mr. Clair, proceeding with a rapid pace again.

During the early part of the month of March, the nights are often very cold; and this particular night was no exception to the general rule. A sharp cutting breeze blew from the north-east, whistling round the corners of the streets, and making the swinging signs creak on their rusty hinges.

Alfred Mordent buttoned up his coat to his chin, and walked briskly on, until he reached Bridge-street, into which thoroughfare he turned. The storm which had been threatening all the evening appeared to have passed off. It is true huge masses of black clouds continued to scud rapidly over the heavens, but they were more separated, and even allowed here and there the pale rays of the moon to shine through the rifts.

Mordent, however, appeared to pay no attention to the condition of the sky. About half-way down Bridge-street he stopped before a three-story dwelling, and first glancing around to see that no one was visible in the street, he knocked three times at the front door. In a few moments it was opened, and he glided into the house.

In about five minutes' time the door was re-opened, but instead of the elegant young gentleman who had entered the house, a man of tall stature, enveloped in a large gray cloak, appeared. He appeared to be about ten years older than Mordent, and the lower portion of his face was covered with a heavy black beard. He proceeded along in the direction of Bond-street. He had not gone, however, many yards, before he noticed a man crouching by the side of the wall.

"Is that you, Lester?" exclaimed the man in the gray cloak, in a loud, gruff voice.

"Yes, captain!" replied the person interrogated, in a trembling voice.

"Anything new here?"

"No, captain!"

"Where is the chief of police?"

"I don't know."

"Well, I will tell you—he is in his office, and the mayor of the city is with him. They are plotting together for my arrest to-night. You go and keep a watch on their movements, and if you hear and see anything, come and let me know.

"Where shall I find you?"

"No. 211, Bond-street."

"All right, captain!" replied Lester, and started off on his errand.

The man in the gray cloak watched him for a moment, and then walked on again. Lester, who had started at a rapid pace, when he had got a little distance off, suddenly stopped and concealed himself behind a telegraph post, he then stretched his head forward, and watched the course taken by the man to whom he had just been speaking. He saw him stop before the door of a house, which from its position he knew must be 211.

"He is really going to that house!" said Lester, to himself. "He evidently does not suspect me."

NELLY CLAIR AND ADA MEREDITH CONVERSES ON LOVE MATTERS.

And he hurried to keep his appointment with the chief of police. But it appeared that if Lester had a viligant eye, the man with the gray cloak had one still more vigilant, for not a single manœuvre had escaped him. When he heard him stop behind a telegraph post, a smile of derision moved his lips. Instead of entering the house before which he stopped, he waited in the doorway until the sounds of Lester's retreating footsteps were lost in the distance.

When the last sound had died away, he continued to walk up Bond-street. He

then began to search the houses on each side of the street, and endeavoured by the aid of the gas lamps to discover their numbers. He at last stood before the dwelling he was in search of, and paused a few moments, as if for the purpose of collecting his thoughts. He then cautiously advanced to the front door, and gently turning the handle, discovered that it was not locked. Opening the door without making the slightest sound, he first of all peered into the hall, and finding that it was unoccupied, he glided upstairs, and entering a particular bedroom, he concealed himself beneath an old-fashioned bureau, in which position it will be remembered he was discovered by Miss Clair, on her retiring for the night.

We must now return to the latter young lady, whom, the reader will remember, we left at the close of the last chapter, debating in her own mind what to do when she discovered who was her nocturnal visitor. After sitting still for full five minutes, she suddenly rose up, and walking straight to where the man with the gray cloak was concealed, she exclaimed with extraordinary presence of mind—

"Captain Rodolph, you may come forth."

"You have discovered me, young lady!" said the man in the gray cloak, coming from his hiding-place, and standing up erect before her.

"What is your business here?" exclaimed Ellen in a perfectly firm voice.

"My motive for coming here, Miss Clair," returned Rodolph, in a perfectly polite tone, is simply to have a few minutes conversation with you, and if you had not spoken first to me, in another minute I should have addressed you."

"You appear to have chosen a strange place for an interview, sir," said Ellen, with a shade of sarcasm in her tone.

"I have to apologise for invading the sancitity of a lady's chamber," said Rodolph, "but it was the only possible means I had of seeing you alone."

"Speak, sir, without wasting any more time—say what you have to say quickly, for this interview can last but a few minutes."

"My visit here, Miss Clair, is simply one of warning. Your father is straining every nerve for my arrest—I came to warn you, as his daughter, that the direst misfortune will fall upon you and yours if he persists in his present course. It will be well for you, Miss Clair, to endeavour to persuade him to cease this persecution."

"Persecution!" interrupted Ellen—"do you call it persecution to endeavour to cause the arrest af a man whose name is associated with every known crime? Is persecution to arrest a robber and murderer?"

"Young lady, you are bold to address such laguage to me, when I have you in my power. You must not believe all you hear concerning Captain Rodolph. But we will not quarrel about words. I will even concede, if you will, that Mr. Clair is only doing his duty by endeavouring to capture me; but I reiterate my warning to you, the most terrible evils will befal you if he continues this course, and I recommend you to use your influence with him to make him give up this pursuit."

"Captain Rodolph," said Ellen, drawing herself up to her full height, "you must indeed think that we are the veriest cowards that ever crawled upon earth. I despise your threats, sir : so far from their having any influence upon me, they will have the contrary effect. I shall advise my father to redouble his vigilance."

"Young lady, beware what you do ! Captain Rodolph is not accustomed to threaten in vain."

"This is my answer, sir," exclaimed Ellen, and she rushed to the door, and unlocking it before her nocturnal visitor had time to prevent her, she ran into the corridor, and called out in a loud voice, " help, help ! Captain Rodolph is in the house---help !"

The robber stood for a moment thunderstruck ; and then recovering himself, he ran to the door, and exclaimed in a threatning voice :—

"Ellen Clair, you shall bitterly repent this day !"

He then ran to the window, threw it open, and leaped into the garden by means of the roofs of some of the outhouses. He had only just disappeared, when Mr. Clair, aroused by his daughter's cries, made his appearance. In a few hurried words she explained all that had passed, and the strictest search was immediately made for the fugitive., but not the slightest trace of him could be discovered.

In the meantime, Captain Rodolph gained the street, and directed his steps with rapid strides towards the eastern portion of the city. He traversed a large number of narrow streets, and at last entered one which was only lighted here and there by a glimmering lamp. He appeared, however, to be perfectly familiar with it, and walked along it until he had reached about the centre. He then stopped before an old tumble-down looking house, and knocked in a peculiar manner, Almost directly afterwards the faint tinkling of a bell reached his ears. He no sooner heard it, than he stooped down, and applying his lips to the key-hole, whispered the words—

"*Three in One !*"

The door was immediately opened, and the man in the gray cloak glided into the house.

----

## CHAPTER VIII.

### THE PRAIRIE.

IT is the privilege of authors to make very long journeys in a very short space of time. Availing ourselves of this privilege, we now transport our readers to one of the great north-western prairies. The time is five months after the events related in the last chapter. It is the middle of the month of August, and the burning sun shines overhead without a single cloud to mitigate his fierce beams. A long drought has evidently prevailed, for the prairie grass is parched and withered, and as far as the eye can reach, it presents the same unbroken brown aspect.

This prairie resembles all others; there was the same level surface, the same boundless view, the same absence of trees, the same unvarying prospect that is to be found in every prairie, no matter what state it may be,

It was about four o'clock in the afternoon of this hot August day, that a solitary horseman was riding through the parched grass. He was an exceedingly handsome young man, of about twenty-four years of age. He was strongly built, and his face was browned by the sun and exposure. He was clothed as an Indian chief, and besides a heavy rifle, which he carried slung across his back, he carried in his belt a brace of Colt's revolvers. Across his saddle was slung the body of a panther. The animal had evidently been recently killed, for the blood still dropped from a wound in the head where the rifle ball had entered.

Although the sun burnt so fiercely, the horseman held himself erect in his saddle, and he did not appear to be in the slightest degree overcome by the temperature. For two hours he continued to walk his horse in a straight line through the long dry grass, without either turning to the right or the left. During his progress, he started deer, prairie-hens, and even jackals and hœnas; but the horseman manifested no desire to hunt game; his indifference even went so far, that he did not deign to cast a single look at them as they went bounding before him.

He came at last to the bed of a river, which, although dried up, offered a better path for his tired steed than the prairie, so he proceeded between the two banks. Suddenly, just as he was about to turn, a bend made by the course of the water, he stopped, and listened attentively. One of those sounds which men accustomed to prairie life can never mistake, reached his ears. He had recognized in the distance the sound of a horse's foot on the hard ground of the bed of the river.

This horseman who had not paid the slightest attention to the wild beast and game which fled at his approach, no sooner heard the sound revealing the presence of a human being than he placed his rifle within his reach, and examined his pistols to see that the caps were all right.

In the desert, as everywhere else, man is the most dangerous animal to be met with

The horseman had not long to wait. Perhaps he was advancing, was ignorant of the presence of another, or perhaps he was so confident in his own strength that he did not concern himself about it. Every moment the sound of the horse's feet grew nearer, and soon the horse and its rider appeared round the bend of the river.

The new comer was a person of tall stature; he was thin, strong, and wiry; his skin was copper colour, and he was dressed as an Indian warrior. His eyes were intensely black, and had a peculiar fascinating power about them. When he saw the first horseman standing motionless before him, he stopped in his turn, for the passage was scarcely wide enough for both to pass abreast. The two men gazed on each other for a moment in silence, when the elder one, who appeared to be much the older of the two, commenced a conversation. Bowing his head in the most graceful manner, he exclaimed, in the Sioux language—

"The Sioux chief in the name of the great spirit, bids you welcome."

"The Ottawa brave thanks his brother," replied the young Indian, in the same language.

"Does my brother travel to the settlement of the pale faces?" asked the Sioux chief.

"He goes where fate leads him."

"Then my brother does not make any special journey?"

"No, he is merely on the hunting path," and the young man pointed to the panther lying across his saddle.

"If you are a born Indian," said the Sioux, "you will do me a favour."

"I am not a born Indian," replied the young man, smiling; "but still, I will do anything to assist you in my power."

"How! you are not an Indian?" cried the Sioux.

"No!"

"What are you, then?"

"I am a pale face."

The young man uttered these words in a proud voice, and placed his hand on one of his pistols, as if he feared an attack; but the other horseman gazed on him with an air of astonishment, and examined him from head to foot.

"Do you speak English?" said he, in that tongue.

"Of course I do," replied the young man, in the same language.

"What countryman are you?"

"That is more than I can tell," replied the young man, smiling. "If you can inform me, you will render me an immense service."

The elder horseman appeared to be a prey to great emotion. His bowed face visibly paled, and his eyes, when he raised them to heaven, appeared filled with tears.

"O God!" he murmured, in a low voice, "thy power is infinite, thy goodness inexhaustible, and I have never doubted Thee. But if thy hand has now conducted me so marvellously into the right path, I shall believe myself the instrument of thy will, and shall no longer hesitate to act."

The junior horseman could not understand the sense of these words, but he saw the look of devotion that his strange companion cast up to heaven. The latter, having finished his almost mute prayer, resumed his natural tone.

"A moment ago," said he, continuing the conversation in English, "I asked a favour of you. I thought by your costume and general appearance, that you were an Indian, and in all probability you took me for one too! But like you, I am a pale face."

"Is it possible?" replied the young man, in a tone of amazement, no doubt surprised at the circumstance that two white men disguised as Indians, should meet together in the middle of the prairie. "If I offered to do anything I could for you supposing you to be an Indian, with how much more alacrity shall I do it, knowing that you are one of my own race? What can I do for you?"

"For ten hours my horse and myself have been travelling without finding a drop of water. Could you direct us to some spring where we can find water and a place to repose, for we are almost dead with thirst and fatigue?"

"Easily! half an hour's travel from here there is a spring, where it is my intention to pass the night. You must have passed close by it on your road here, but it is so concealed that it might easily have escaped your notice. In order to reach it you have only to turn back, and as the bed of this stream will not allow us to pass each other, if you are afraid of going ahead of me, we can exchange horses."

"I am not afraid," replied the other.

But before adopting the suggestion made by the young man, he looked at him again with that extraordinary, scrutinizing glance of which we have before spoken.

"Your name, young man?" said he, in a tone of voice so gentle, that it inspired the young horseman's respect.

"I have two names," he replied; "those who live on the prairie, call me Eagle Eye."

"And your other name?"

"O!" said the young man with a me-lancholy air, "I cannot tell why I believe that other name to be mine. I cannot even tell how it is, that it remains engraved on my memory. I am entirely ignorant of who gave it me. I do not know where I lived when I was called thus. It may merely be the illusion of a dream."

"But what is the name?" asked his companion, in a voice revealing the most vivid curiosity.

"Do you really want to know it?"

"I do, indeed. What is it?"

"Alfred!" replied the young horseman.

"Alfred!" repeated the other, bending his head to the ground, while a deep flush succeeded his former pallor. He remained speechless for a few moments, and then raising his head, he gazed again on the young man's face. But his glance had lost all its rigidity and coldness, and had almost a tender expression. At last he withdrew his eyes, and turning his horse in the narrow path, he proceeded along the bed of the river, followed step by step by the younger horseman.

Not a word passed between them for a considerable time. They both appeared to be reflecting on the strangeness of their meeting. The elder horseman was plunged into the most profound reverie. Every now and then his lips moved, and an observer would suppose he was addressing a prayer to heaven.

"It is he! it is he!" he murmured to himself, turning half round in his saddle to observe the young man, who followed him at a short distance. "God's mercy is infinite! After having searched so long, and at the very moment when hope abandoned me, to find myself face to face with him in the midst of this vast prairie! It almost supasses belief."

The young man to whom the Indians had given the fanciful name of Eagle Eye, also indulged in his own reflections, awakened by the presence of the stranger. He said nothing, however, but pursued his way silently. They proceeded in this manner, until the river made a new turn, which they had no sooner rounded, than they saw it was divided into two streams; both, however, now dry. The first horseman was about proceeding straight on, when Alfred cried out;

"Turn to the right. We shall find the spring about a hundred yards from here."

The horseman followed the direction given without making any reply, and the two men soon found themselves side by side, on the prairie again. Exactly facing them was a thicket of brushwood, situated at the bottom of a slight descent. It was a veritable green oasis in the midst of the parched up vegetation.

At the moment the horsemen reached

the charming green spot, the sun was rapidly sinking in the west, tinging the whole horizon with its glorious dying beams. Soon an almost insensible undulation of the leaves of the shrubbery indicated that an evening breeze was setting in. Even the horses were sensible of its refreshing influence, and neighed joyously as it cooled their panting and smoking flanks. They had already penetrated into the middle of the shrubbery, when suddenly the horse of the elder rider fell back on its haunches, while its dilated nostrils showed that it was under the influence of some sudden fear. The horseman leaned forward to see what it was, and saw a small animal about the size of a young cat rolling on the green grass.

"Beware!" he cried in a loud voice to his younger companion. "There's a panther here."

He had scarcely finished, when a formidable roar filled the air, and a female panther of immense size started up from the foot of a tree where it had been reclining, and placed herself directly in their path. For a moment both horses and men appeared to be undecided what to do; but Alfred soon decided on his course of action. He raised his rifle rapidly to his shoulder, and before a word could be spoken, he had sent the unerring ball into the wild animal's brain. The elder horseman had remained perfectly motionless, watching with a searching eye every action of his young companion.

"Intrepid and calm," he murmured; "he is really his father's son."

Alfred jumped off his horse, and without paying the slightest attention to the panther, he took off the saddle and bridle from his steed, and allowed it to crop the grass which abounded in that spot. His companion followed his example, and they both penetrated a little further into the brushwood, until they came to the edge of a clear running brook, around which the grass was green and soft.

"We can take our ease here," said the young man, throwing himself on the ground, and dipping a leathern cup into the pellucid stream, handed it overflowing with sweetness to his thirsty companion. The latter emptied it at a single draught, and then threw himself on the grass sward beside Alfred.

"You speak English well," said he. "Of what country are you?"

"I was born in the city of York—but is it possible that you do not know where you were born?"

"I only know that I am not an Indian, although I speak their language as well as they do themselves."

"But who taught you English?"

"I do not know. It is the language of my infancy—since then, I have learnt Indian."

"But—your parents?"

"My parents," repeated Alfred, "I have no recollection of them."

"But do you remember nothing of your childhood's days?"

"Nothing definite; everything is vague. I remember being sick, and having my head bandaged up. I have some indistinct recollection of a terrible shock."

"Young man," said the elder horseman, "be kind enough to bare your left arm."

Alfred did as he was requested, and rolling up the sleeve of his coat, revealed a large white scar a little above the wrist.

His companion examined it with much attention, and then muttered a few words to himself, in a supressed voice.

"But what kind of a life have you led?" he exclaimed, after a moment's pause.

"I have led a wandering life—my earliest definite recollections are of an Indian village—and I sometimes think that I must have been born amongst the Indians."

"What is your age now?"

"I am twenty-three years of age."

While this conversation had been going on, Alfred had been preparing their frugal repast. It was now ready, and they both did ample justice to it. It began to grow dark. The sky was beautifully clear, and thousands of stars peeped out from the clear blue ether.

"You know the country you say?" said the young man, re-commencing the conversation, which had been interrupted by their meal.

"Yes, I know every portion of it—and one of the most beautiful neighbourhoods is Clinton."

When he mentioned this place, the elder horseman fixed his eyes on Alfred's face—but the latter betrayed no sign of recognition.

"Clinton," said the young man, repeating the name as if for the first time in his life.

"Yes, I had a dear friend who lived near there. His house was called Mordent Grange."

"Mordent Grange!" exclaimed the young man, quickly. "I have certainly heard that name before. But perhaps some traveller has mentioned it to me."

"It is a beautiful mansion, situate on the brow of one of the mountains. The Schuylkill river runs near it, and the country round it is very picturesque. There is a terrible precipice a short distance up the mountain."

"How strange!" said the young man, pressing his fingers to his forehead—"it seems to me that I have seen this house in my dreams."

"The gentleman who lived on this estate," continued the other, watching the effects of his story on Alfred's face, "was named Mordent—but I tire you, perhaps?"

"No, indeed," replied Alfred, "your story has an attraction for me which I cannot account for. Go on, if you please ; tell me all about this house and its inhabitants. You say the gentleman who lived there was your friend?"

"Yes."

"Is he still alive?"

"No, he was basely murdered."

"Tell me the particulars!"

"I must first of all tell you my name—it is George Percival, and Mordent was my bosom friend."

Mr. Percival related to the young man all the particulars which we have before given to the reader, in the first chapters of this history, and which it is not necessary we should repeat.

"Your story interests me strangely," said Alfred ; "you said a little while ago that you received a mysterious warning of this assassination, but you did not tell me what it was?"

"I was living in the city at the time, engaged in scientific pursuits, when one night a horrible dream disturbed my sleep. I thought I saw Mr. Mordent struggling with an assassin—this dream was repeated three times —and I could no longer resist the appeal, but that very night started off for Mordent Grange. I did not reach there until the middle of the next day. I arrived too late, my friend had been killed the night before."

"But what became of Mrs. Mordent and the child?"

"The villain who had committed the deed, seized the child in his arms, and rushed up the mountain with it, followed by the frantic mother. He arrived at the edge of a precipice—"

"And threw the child into the gulf?" interrupted Alfred.

"Yes, and the mother, bereft of her senses at the sight, plunged headlong after it."

"It is strange—very strange," said the young man, leaning his forehead on his hand. He then rose up, and began to walk hurriedly up and down.

"It appears to me," he said, "that I have heard this story before, and that I am in some way mixed up with it. Was anything ever heard of the child afterwards?" he added, turning to Mr. Percival.

"Yes. A traveller early on the morning of the day that I arrived there, when passing the precipice, heard a child moaning, and looking down, saw an infant lodged in the midst of some shrubbery, about ten feet from the surface. He rescued the infant—but from that day to this, nothing more has been

heard of it. I have made a vow that I will discover him—and for that purpose, for the last three years I have traversed nearly over the whole world."

"What was the name of the villain who committed this fearful deed?"

"A name well known ; Captain Rodolph."

"Have you succeeded in finding any trace of the party you seek?"

"I think I have."

The young man fixed an earnest look upon his companion, as if he would read his very thoughts. The latter continued his relation : - "After the death of my friend and his wife, I devoted myself entirely to scientific pursuits, and in furtherance of my studies, I took up my abode in London. I remained there fifteen years. I then returned. What was my extreme surprise to learn that a young man who claimed to be Mr. Mordent's missing son, had brought an action at law for the recovery of his father's property! The evidence he produced was very strong. Several of his father's old servants recognized him. He was able to give a distinct account of his life from the time he stated he was rescued from the gulf. According to his statement, he had been kept a prisoner for fifteen years, by the same parties that had taken his father's life, and that at length he had escaped from them. The young man in the course of the trial, stoutly maintained that it was Captain Rodolph who had committed the fearful deed—but a band of horse-thieves, and that he had been compelled to wander about the country with them. There was one witness, however, who stated that he did not see the slightest resemblance between the claimant and Mr. Mordent's son ; this witness was named Robert Bartol, and had been the little boy's playmate from his birth. The jury, after a long deliberation, returned a verdict for the claimant, and he was reinstated into the estates of his supposed father."

"But," interruped Alfred, "I do not understand how it is you should be seeking for Mr. Mordent's son, if he has already been found?"

"Hear me out, and you will be no longer surprised. When I heard all these particulars, I thought as you do, that the long lost child had been found, and intoxicated with joy and happiness, I resolved to pay him a visit at Mordent Grange. The young man received me with the utmost politeness, but he did not recognize the friend of his childhood, either by name or appearance. This did not surprise me, for children five years of age rarely remember in after life the companions of their infancy. But there were two things about this young man, which struck me with extreme surprise. The first was, that his hair was as black as ebony, while a lock of the hair of the child which the mother had given me only a few months before her melancholy death, was almost flaxen. The second cause of surprise was, that I did not trace the slightest resemblance or feature to the young child I knew. But when I came to reflect on the matter, my surprise was mitigated; the phenomenon of light hair in infancy and black hair at puberty, is a common one, and features often change with age. I again went over the proofs, and came to the conclusion, that had I been on the jury, I should have given the same verdict."

"Then he was really Mr. Mordent's son?" said Alfred.

"My dear young friend," returned Mr. Percival—"I entreat you to hear me out. I remained some weeks at Mordent Grange; but I soon perceived that my presence was disagreeable to my host, and I resolved to return home. This young heir inspired me with a disagreeable impression, or rather an antipathy, whereas, the child had inspired me with love and affection. I was compelled to acknowledge that young Mordent was intelligent—but under this intelligence, I saw that he had a cold, egotistical and cruel heart. I left Mordent Grange, determined to devote myself more closely than ever to study—and I had no sooner reached my own house, than I entered with ardour into various experiments of a highly interesting character."

Mr. Percival here paused. Alfred had listened to him with the most profound attention, his countenance exhibiting at the same time both hope and anxiety. When he saw that the speaker had ceased, this expression was succeeded by one of mournful indifference.

"Well, after all," said he, "it appears that he was really Mr. Mordent's son. He has come into possession of his name and fortune—he is rich and happy. It appears to me, that your mission is entirely accomplished."

"Not yet!" said Percival, suddenly rising to his feet.

"How not yet?"

"That Mr. Mordent's son exists, I am certain; but he has not yet come into possession of his father's property, nor even his father's name."

"What! Is all that you have just told me only a fable?"

"Undoubtedly not."

"But explain?"

"That there is a young man who is called Mordent, and that he enjoys the fortune left by Mr. Mordent, of Mordent Grange, by the decision of a court of law, is true," replied Mr. Percival, in a ringing voice—"but what is still more true is, that this man is an impostor—that he has succeeded to this property by means of false witnesses—that he is not the son of Henry and Catherine Mordent!"

Alfred stood as if thunderstruck; a strange emotion caused his limbs to tremble, and his face to grow ashy white.

"But this son—the real son—where and who is he?" he asked, in a hoarse voice.

"This son," repeated Mr. Percival, his piercing eyes lighting up with a strange fire —"this son, whose existence science has proved to me, and whom I have been seeking for three years, has a scar on his left arm, a little above the wrist."

And without giving time for Alfred to make any reply, he seized the young man's arm and again revealed the scar.

"Alfred Mordent," said Mr. Percival, "let us thank God together, for it is he who has led me to you."

They both fell on their knees and offered up a prayer to the Ruler of the universe.

---

## CHAPTER IX.

### THE LOCK OF HAIR.

IT was some little time before Alfred appeared to realize the fact that he was the long lost son, and that an imposter had deprived him of his birthright.

"Am I awake, or am I dreaming?" he exclaimed. "Am I really the son of that noble man who was so basely assassinated?'

"You are really and truly his son," replied Mr. Percival.

"But—the proofs—the proofs?"

"The proofs abound—but unfortunately at present they are only conclusive to my mind. Listen to me, young man. Before I give you the proofs you demand, you must know how I discovered the claimant for the Mordent estates was an imposter. These details are necessary, that you may know the enemies with whom you have to combat, their power and deceit. Sit down near me and listen."

Mr. Percival threw himself on the grass, and with a gesture invited Alfred to sit beside him. The young man, swayed by hope and fear, obeyed mechanically. After a few minutes' silence, the elder traveller resumed:

"I have already told you," said he, "that all my life I have been a student. I have dabbled in all the sciences, especially those of an occult character. Three years ago, while pursuing my investigations, I became acquainted with an old man named Ralph Tryon, the possessor of an original and powerful mind. I could not even guess his age, but in the first instance there was something about him which caused me to feel repugnance towards him; but after a little time, I got accustomed to him, the love of science causing me to subdue my natural antipathies. Our special study together was animal magnetism; and many were the discoveries we made. The great difficulty, however, which we had to contend with, was the want of a proper subject—this want, however, was afterwards supplied in rather a strange manner."

"But do you not believe in magnetism ?" interrupted Alfred.

"I believe, Alfred, in a great many things which to your uneducated mind would appear very ridiculous ; but science familiarizes everything to us. But let me continue my story. One day a poor weak German girl came begging at my house for alms. She was about fifteen years of age, beautiful as an angel. I gave her shelter and a home. She was grateful, and appeared to regard me with filial affection. I noticed that when she turned her large, dreamy eyes upon me, she appeared absorbed in an inexplicable ecstacy. The thought suddenly occurred to me, that she might be a good subject for mesmeric experiment. I tried her, and found her more susceptible than any one I had ever seen before. There was a jealousy between Ralph Tryon and myself. He had never seen Minna—for so my protege was called—and I determined he never should."

"But what were the results of your experiments ?" asked Alfred.

"You shall know by-and-by," continued Mr. Percival ; "but I must tell my story in my own way. Ralph Tryon lived, and lives still, I believe, in an old house situated in East Street, which he has fitted up as an extensive laboratory, and prosecutes his researches with unremitting ardour One evening when we were working together in his apartments, Tryon, from some motive of which I was ignorant, became communicative and confidential, and informed me that he had an extraordinary man on a visit to him, who was willing to join his labours to ours ; but, he added further, that he was a strange personage—and from some whim of his own, he would insist upon keeping his face concealed by a mask, and he finally concluded by offering to introduce me to him. This explanation and these details were all unnecessary. Of course I understood that the old man concealed the truth from me, but curiosity impelled me on, and I accepted his offer. He at once led me into a magnificent laboratory, and I found there a man with a mask on at work. Tryon then introduced me into two other laboratories, and in each of them I found the same personage. I could not be 'deceived, and yet one would have supposed they were three distinct men ; for their occupation was different from each other. In the first laboratory I recognized a chemist making numerous experiments, the nature of which would lead one to suppose that he was an alchemist rather than a modern chemist. In the second laboratory I found a mechanic endowed with extraordinary ability. In the third, a man possessing an intelligence so vast, that it embraced all the different branches of science known to humanity. His particular study,

however, appeared to be electricity. This chemist, this mechanic, this man of science was named Reynolds. His face was so carefully concealed by a mask, that I could not even guess his features."

"But what you tell me," interrupted Alfred, "is so incredible in this nineteenth century, as to be almost beyond belief."

"Incredible or not," replied Mr. Percival, "it is true. I soon understood why I had been introduced to this man. My long and constant studies rendered my assistance an object—and it was arranged that we should meet together on the second Saturday of each month, for the purpose of prosecuting our studies. For my own part I recognized in this stranger a superior intelligence, and I rejoiced that chance had thrown us together. Still I felt a curiosity to know who this man was, and one evening I interrogated Minna while she was asleep as to this personage. The young girl, ordinarily very easily impressed, found great difficulty in replying to my question. At last, constrained by my will, she replied :

"'This man is the son of Ralph Tryon.'

"'His son !' I cried, surprised at this unexpected revelation. I then asked Minna why he wished us to be acquainted ? She replied that Tryon wished to perfect his son in knowledge, and that he knew he could obtain from me important information. She then suddenly exhibited great uneasiness, and added that I must be on my guard, that great danger threatened me—that she could not tell in what the danger consisted ; but that it would emanate from the masked man and his father. More and more astonished, I pressed Minna to inform me why Tryon concealed from me his relationship with the masked man, and who Tryon really was, for I was satisfied that his name was an assumed one. Minna made no reply. By no effort of mine could I make her speak, although I tortured the poor girl by the force of my will. At last, breathless and exhausted, she begged for rest.

"I insist on your answering my questions," I cried.

"'I cannot,' replied Minna, writhing as if she were in a convulsion.

"'Why ?'

"'I cannot see. I cannot see.'

"'What is necessary to make you see ?'

"'I must be put into direct communication with those whose thoughts you wish me to know.'

"'Then they must be here in the same room with you ?'

"'Yes.'

"'Is there no other means by which you can tell the thoughts of these men without seeing them ?'

"'Yes, there is another method—'

"'What is it ?'

"'Give me something that has belonged

ADA MEREDITH.

"Yes, father."

"Open the cage."

Hubert fell back in perfect stupefaction.

"Open Bacchus's cage !" he cried, as if he had not heard aright.

"Yes," replied the old man, in a quiet tone of voice.

"Open Bacchus's cage !" repeated Hubert for the second time.

"Exactly what I mean."

"But, father—"

"Did you not tell me that nothing had any effect on him ?"

"Certainly I did."

MYSTERIOUS MAN.—No. 6.

"Well, I want to prove to you that you only wanted force of will to effect your purpose."

"But—"

"Did you not give up the task of taming him ?"

"Yes."

"Well, then, I will tame him ; I, an old man, nearly eighty years of age. Open that cage, Hubert, I order it."

The young man still hesitated.

"Did you not hear me ?" cried the old man, in an angry voice. "Open that cage, I command it."

# PUBLISHER'S NOTE

Missing Pages 33-40.

Hubert, subdued by the imperious voice in which this order was pronounced, approached the cage, and drew back the two bolts which closed the door. Ralph Tryon threw it open, and entered the cage. The tiger, in face of this unexpected invasion, stood still, and, doubtlessly stupified by the old man's audacity, he fixed on him his dilated eyes and growled angrily.

Without noticing these threatening signs, Tryon advanced with his forefinger extended, and with his eyes fixed on those of the ferocious beast. At every step the old man made, the tiger fell back. At last he reached the extremity of his cage; he then reared up, and appeared ready to spring on his bold visitor.

Hubert with his eyes fixed seemed nailed to the spot, and appeared fascinated by the terrible spectacle being enacted before his eyes.

Tryon still continued to advance until his feet came in contact with the tiger's paws. Then augmenting so to say the dominating power of his look, he slowly bent down, still keeping his eyes fixed on those of the animal, and seizing the beast by the throat, he dragged it by sheer muscular strength into the middle of the cage. The tamed tiger remained motionless, his muscles were relaxed, and he seemed to be completely prostrated. Tryon now sat down on the animal's shoulders, and seizing its jaws with his two hands opened them wide, and showed its red mouth garnished with formidable rows of teeth.

Hubert could not prevent a cry of surprise, admiration, and fear from escaping him. The old man paid no attention to it —he appeared to be entirely absorbed by the examination of the mouth of the animal.

"He has not finished teething yet," said he, slowly, "and that is the cause of my poor Bacchus's attacks of rage. But before a month has passed, I will render him as gentle as the most faithful dog."

The old man picked up the iron rod which he had let fall, and rose up from off the animal's back. By this movement, however, Bacchus escaped from the dominion of his eye; with a single bound he rose to his feet, and prepared to make a spring.

Tryon turned abruptly round.

"Down!" cried he, in an angry voice; and again his eyes caught those of the tiger, and the animal crouched at his feet completely subdued.

Ralph Tryon raised the iron rod, and inflicted a heavy blow on the beast's shoulders; the latter uttered a growl of pain, while the old man walked majestically out of the cage.

"Father," cried Hubert, "you are my master, nothing is impossible with you. I recognise my own weakness, and testify to your power."

"Now," replied Tryon, "you can henceforth enter boldly into Bacchus's cage—and soon he will allow you take any liberty with him. But come, let us go into your workshop that I may examine your work."

So saying, he led the way to the door by which Hubert and the dogs had entered.

---

## CHAPTER XII.
### THE SECRET.

THE apartment into which the father and son now penetrated, was fitted up as a workshop, where every possible kind of labour appeared to be carried on. Turning lathes, machines of all kinds, every description of carpenter's tools, such as hammers, chisels, centre-pieces, &c., were strewn all around. But what would strike the observer as being in the greatest profusion, were the burglar's instruments which met him at every turn.

Lion and Shadrac lay side by side on the ground. When the two men entered the workshop, Lion opened his eyes, and then closed them again, Shadrac rolled on his back, which appeared to be his favourite position. The old man examined very carefully various machines in process of construction, and expressed himself as very much pleased with them. They had been in the room but a few minutes when a shrill whistle was heard to break the silence which reigned in the workshop.

"It is *he!*" murmured Tryon; "it is *he!*" Then turning to Hubert, he added: "You love Ellen, the daughter of the chief of police?"

"Yes, father."

"It is your intention to carry her off?"

"Yes, father."

"Swear to me, whatever may be your love for this young girl, that you will never oppose my wishes?"

"I swear it, father."

A second whistle, still louder and more shrill than the first, was now heard.

"It is *he!*" again exclaimed Tryon. "Hold yourself in readiness," he added, turning to Hubert. "Perhaps I shall want you."

When he had finished speaking, the old man opened the door, and again entered the menagerie.

"He has come," he muttered to himself, as he walked. "Let him once give me the benefit of his knowledge, and I will laugh at the whole world."

At that moment he found himself opposite the tiger's cage. Bacchus looked at him fixedly. The old man stopped, and again fixed his glance as before on the ferocious beast. The latter, entirely subdued, lowered his head and retreated to the wall.

"The influence is manifest," murmured

Tryon—"cannot the same influence be brought to bear on man who is much more feebly organised?"

He now passed rapidly on, and re-entered the chemical laboratory where he had left his son Vivian. The latter standing motionless beside the furnace.

"Where is he?" asked Tryon, in an abrupt tone.

"There," replied Vivian, pointing to the door by which the old man had entered.

"With Reynold?"

"Yes, father."

"Was he alone?"

"No father."

"Who accompanied him?"

"I do not know."

"How! you do not know?"

"The person who accompanied him was covered with a long veil, which entirely concealed her."

"He did not see you?"

"No—I was careful of your instructions, and concealed myself when he entered. He went straight to Reynold's room, followed by the person of whom I have spoken."

"So," murmured Ralph Tryon, "he has not deceived me—he has kept his promise—I will keep mine;" then turning to Vivian, he added, "go on with your work, but remember my orders, and hold yourself in readiness."

Vivian bowed, and obeyed the command given him by his father. The latter left the apartment, and directed his steps to the third door in the corridor, and opening it as he had done the others, he crossed the threshold.

---

In order to make the reader understand properly what is to follow, it is necessary that we should go back an hour or two in our history. Exactly as the clock struck ten, Mr George Percival, accompanied by a young girl, left his home, and calling a carriage, ordered the driver to proceed to East Street. When he had reached this point, he dismissed the vehicle, and proceeded on foot up East Street, and stopped before Ralph Tryon's house. He now took the young girl by the hand, and knocked on the door three times. It was opened almost immediately by the old woman of whom we have before spoken, and they both entered.

The door had no sooner closed on them, than Mr Percival made several passes over the young girl's face, and she immediately sunk into a state of insensibility. He raised her in his arms and bore her straight to Tryon's study. He appeared to know all the secrets of the house, for he walked straight to that portion of the wall through which we saw the old man disappear, and touching she secret spring, the panel rolled back, revealing the secret staircase. He descended these rapidly and the panel closed as before. At last he stood before Reynold's chamber, and blew a whistle which he took from his pocket. He had no sooner done this, than the door opened and he entered.

The chamber into which he penetrated exactly resembled Hubert's workshop, but it was furnished in an entirely different manner. Three chandeliers extending from the ceiling lighted it up brilliantly. The walls of this apartment were lined with books, and a centre-table was covered with papers, manuscripts, and unbound volumes. Several powerful electric machines and galvanic batteries stood in various parts of the room, while divers Leyden jars on the chimney-piece would seem to indicate that the inmate devoted his attention to electricity and its sister sciences.

When Mr Percival entered the room, a man was standing beside the table, the elasticity of whose limbs still showed youth. His features, like those of Vivian and Hubert, were concealed by a mask. There was one thing that was very strange about him, and that was that the height, motions, and general appearance of this third inhabitant of the mysterious house were identical with the other two we have already introduced to the reader; that is to say, that the extraordinary resemblance we have referred to before as existing between Vivian and Hubert, also existed in the case of the occupant of this apartment. This resemblance was so perfect, that any one would declare that they were all three one and the same person.

Mr Percival advanced into the middle of the chamber, still holding in his arms the form of the unconscious girl. He placed his burden on a sofa standing in a recess.

"What have you there?" asked Reynold, to the new comer.

"Something that I shall require to-night."

"What is it? A corpse?"

"Look for yourself."

When he uttered these last words, Percival's face assumed an ironical expression, and he cast a searching look on the inmate of the chamber. Reynold approached the sofa, and removing the long veil which enveloped Minna's form, he gazed on her pale face. A cry of horror, stupor, and anger escaped him, and his trembling hands let go the veil he had seized. The body was that of a young girl apparently deprived of life, who seemed to be about eighteen years of age, and who was beautiful in every acceptation of the word. Her hair was a golden auburn, her forehead a pure white, her eyes a celestial blue, while her teeth might rival a necklace of pearls without spot or blemish. Her cheeks were pale, her eyes open, but there was no expression of life to be traced in her face, the set muscles of which gave her that appearance of quietude and repose peculiar to the dead.

Reynold, after he had given utterance to the cry of horror, remained motionless as if he had been struck by lightning. At last he turned towards Percival with an expression of fury in his face impossible to be described.

"It is she !" he cried.

"Yes," replied Percival, paying no attention to the speaker's threatening tone. "It is she herself, Reynold. You see I have discovered what you tried so earnestly to conceal ?"

"Is she dead ?" asked Reynold, appearing not to have heard the speaker's last words.

"Do you think so ?" replied Percival smiling.

Reynold, without making any reply, placed his hand successively on the young girl's arm and over the region of her heart.

"The body is yet warm," he exclaimed in a hoarse voice. "There is no wound to be seen, but her heart no longer beats. Oh, if you have killed her, Percival, you have committed a fearful crime, and woe be to you !"

"You love her then ?"

"Do I love her ?" replied Reynold, his eyes gleaming forth a strange fire ; "yes, I love her, and if you have killed her—"

The door of the apartment suddenly opening, interrupted the young man, and Ralph Tryon entered the room. When Reynold saw the old man, he receded, while the nervous trembling which agitated his body bore witness to the effort he had been obliged to make to restrain the anger and emotion which had taken possession of him.

Without appearing to notice the presence of Percival, nor that of the man in the mask, Tryon walked straight to the couch where the young girl was extended without motion. He leaned over her with visible anxiety painted on his face. He then turned around to her reputed father.

"What is the result ?" said he.

"I have made the attempt," replied the visitor.

"With what success," again asked the old man.

"I have only half succeeded."

"Then you have only obtained—"

"What you see—a lethargic sleep."

"The body then obeys you ?"

"Yes, but with difficulty."

"But the mind ?"

"I have no power over the mind."

"Do you know why you have not succeeded ?"

"Why ?"

"Because your will has not been sufficiently strong."

Percival regarded the old man with an expression of disdainful pity.

"Try what you can do," said he.

Reynold listened without moving to this strange conversation. His eyes remained fixed on the young girl's prostrate form, and it appeared as if nothing could withdraw him from this mute contemplation.

"She is not dead ?" suddenly exclaimed Reynold—"life is returning ; she has just moved."

"Her lethargic sleep is passing off," said Percival.

"I willed that she should wake," said Tryon, in a proud tone of voice.

Whatever might be the cause, whether her sleep ceased naturally, or whether it was owing to any influence on her mind, the young girl made a slight movement with her head, then closed her beautiful eyes, and then opened them again almost immediately. Reynold advanced, and passing his right arm round her supple waist, assisted her to her feet.

"Leave her alone ! Go away !" cried the young man's father, pushing him violently on one side ; "you interfere with the currents by your contact. Rise ! walk ! awake ! I will it !" continued the old man, in a voice of command.

The young girl made an effort to walk, but she tottered as if she would fall to the ground.

"Your influence interferes with mine," said the old man, addressing his visitor. "You have caused the body to sleep, wake it—I will take care of the mind."

Percival placed his hands on the young girl's forehead, and uttered a few words in a low tone of voice. Minna stood up and opened her eyes. She surveyed the chamber at first with a vague look, but it soon became more assured, and then she contemplated fixedly the objects which surrounded her.

"Where am I ?" said she, in a sweet voice.

"Let her take a little repose," said Percival to Tryon, who had stretched out his hands to seize those of the young girl.

"Why ?"

"Because she is too much fatigued."

"What matter ?"

"She may not be able to bear a second crisis, and you might kill her."

"What matter ?" repeated for the second time the unpitying old man.

"You wish it, then ?"

"Yes."

"Well, then, do as you will."

Percival let go Tryon's arm, and the latter advanced towards Minna. Reynold turned abruptly, almost violently, to the visitor, and pointed to Minna.

"Who is that young girl ?" he asked.

"Silence ?" said Tryon, in an angry voice.

"Who is that girl ?—I will know," said Reynold, in a decided voice.

"That young girl belongs to me," said Percival, coldly.

"To you?"

"Yes."

"Is she your daughter?"

"What business is that of yours?"

"Silence, I tell you!" exclaimed Tryon, seizing Minna's hands, and gazing earnestly into her eyes.

"I will have my question answered!" cried Reynold, his face turning purple with anger. "From whence comes this girl?"

Percival slowly crossed his arms over his chest, and regarded Reynold with a disdainful look. He did not, however, intimidate the latter.

"That girl is mine, Reynold," replied the visitor, in that grave and disdainful tone which seemed peculiar to him. "That girl, I repeat, is mine—let that suffice you, and do not forget that you are speaking to your masters."

"My masters!" repeated Reynold, proudly raising his head—"my masters!"

"Silence! I command it," repeated for the third time the old man's imperious voice.

While this conversation had been carried on between Reynold and Percival, Tryon had continued the mesmeric process with the young girl. He had first of all seized her hands and obliged her to take a position in the middle of the chamber. The old man, with his body bent forward, with his face almost touching that of the poor girl, with his forehead very much contracted, with his grinning, toothless mouth, with his eyes horribly dilated, offered a spectacle which was scarcely human. Minna's arms were extended and stiff, as if for the purpose of repulsing her persecutor; her head inclined over one of her shoulders, and she might be compared to a small bird fascinated by a hawk seeing her danger, but utterly unable to escape it. Tryon himself was unrecognisable, a supernatural power seemed to have animated his aged body, and he appeared to be endowed with inexplicable and extraordinary strength. Evidently his mental faculties were so much excited as to place him on the very verge of madness.

This spectacle produced on Reynold and Percival effects of a diametrically opposite character. The latter was cold and impassible—and did not appear to be the least moved by the scene being enacted before him; while Reynold was motionless and stupified, and watched with extraordinary avidity the phenomenon being exhibited in his presence. His mask concealed the expression of his features.

The young girl, completely fascinated, with her eyes closed, her mouth half-open, reclined more and more backwards, until she appeared to be on the point of losing her equilibrium. Reynold, believing she was about to fall, extended his arms to sustain her, but before he could accomplish it, Ralph Tryon abruptly let go of Minna's hands, and made a rapid threatening gesture with his arms.

"Remain in that position!" he exclaimed, in a hoarse voice.

The poor girl remained motionless, but her position was so abnormal, that it appeared as if only a miracle could sustain her in it. In fact, with her head reclining on her right shoulder, with her arms extended forward, with her body bent so far backwards, that her long hair touched the floor, it appeared utterly impossible that she could maintain that position, with the equilibrium necessary to the human body. And yet Tryon no longer sustained her, and she remained in the position without moving, as if all her joints were suddenly ossified. She resembled one of those statues which the caprice of the artist has created during the fever of a diseased imagination.

Tryon, his forehead streaming with perspiration, and with the veins so swollen that they appeared to have been transformed into blue cords, turned triumphantly to his visitor.

"What do you think of it?" said he.

"I have obtained exactly the same result," said Mr Percival. "It is simply lethargy and epilepsy. The body submits to the influence and obeys—but the mind?"

"It will obey as well as the body!" said Tryon, drawing himself up to his full height.

And returning to Minna, he again took her hands. But this time, so far from acting as he had done at first, he now proceeded with gentleness. He now scarcely touched her finger, which he had convulsively grasped before. The body, obeying the influence, assumed a natural position. Tryon now drew a chair towards him, and caused her to sit on it, by simply placing his finger on her forehead. Doubtlessly this action relieved the poor girl, for she allowed a sigh of satisfaction to escape her. Minna's lips opened as if she would speak, but no sound was articulated.

"What is the matter?" said the old man, in a gentle voice.

The young girl conveyed her hand to her throat.

"You suffer?"

"Yes," murmured Minna.

"What can I do?"

"Release me!"

"How?"

"By placing your hands on my throat."

The old man obeyed; the girl breathed more easily. Tryon turned to Percival.

"Her mind is under mesmeric influence," said he.

His visitor made no reply, but some sudden emotion appeared to have take possession of him; he showed it in the marble pallor of his face, and in the peculiar sparkle of his eyes. Tryon, however, was so absorbed in his experiments, that he did not notice the change that had taken place in Percival.

"Do you sleep ?" said he, continuing to question the young girl.

"Yes," she replied.

"An ordinary and natural sleep ? "

"No."

"What kind is it then ?"

"The sleep you have imposed upon me."

"Who has power over you now ?"

"You."

"Whom does your mind obey ?"

"You."

"Can you see into this chamber ?"

"I can see if you will it."

"Can you see out of this chamber ?"

"If you will it."

"Then distance and material objects are annihilated before my will ?"

"Yes."

"Where are you ?"

"In the house of one called Ralph Tryon —but that is not his real name."

The old man trembled, and a slight pallor invaded his face.

"You are wrong," said he.

"No," replied Minna, "I read your thoughts."

"Well, never mind—what house is this in which you are ?"

"It is an old house full of mystery. There are a number of apartments in it—some are used for laboratories and workshops—and there are a number of secret doors in it."

While Minna was speaking, the old man's face was lighted up with proud satisfaction. Then pointing to Reynold, he exclaimed in a loud voice :

"Who is this ?"

Minna at first made no reply to this question. A blush overspread her charming face, and she seemed under the influence of some deep emotion.

"He whom you call Reynold," she replied at last.

"Is not that his name ?"

"Yes, but he has another name."

"Silence !" exclaimed Tryon, in a tone of authority.

"O !" exclaimed the young girl, with a terrible expression of despair and fear painted on her face—"Ah ! I am afraid !"

"Afraid !" exclaimed the old man, astonished. "Why ?"

"Because I see blood !" stammered the somnambulist —"blood ! blood !" she repeated, feebly. "O, I see—I see—I—"

Tryon turned very pale.

"Be silent ! I will it !" said he, abruptly, in a hollow voice.

Scarcely had he uttered these words, when a shudder ran through the poor girl's delicate frame. A fearful change had taken place in her. Frightful convulsions seized her, and she uttered inarticulate cries.

Tryon, stupified, rushed towards her as well as Reynold.

"You kill me ! pity ! pity !" murmured the poor girl, in an accent of despair, impossible to describe.

"Awake ! I will it !" exclaimed Tryon.

But this time the old man's command appeared to have no effect. Her convulsions increased in violence.

"What is the matter with her ?" cried Reynold, seizing her in his arms. "What have you done to her ?"

"Help ! help !" cried the young girl, freeing herself from his grasp. "They are both killing me. For pity sake, deliver me from their influence. One wills, and the other wills not—I cannot—I die !"

And she fell on the seat which she had for the moment abandoned. A cry of rage uttered by Tryon, caused Reynold to turn round. A few steps behind father and son, stood Mr Percival, his face contracted, his arms extended, a strange light gleaming from his eyes, and drawn up to the full majesty of his height.

"She shall speak ! I will it !" he exclaimed. "I will know both your secrets as now you know mine."

And he advanced close to the spot where Minna sat.

"The real name of this man ?" cried he, pointing to Ralph Tryon.

"Silence !" howled the old man. with a horrible expression of countenance.

"His name !" exclaimed Percival, with one hand seizing Tryon and holding him in an iron grasp, while with his other hand he made a rapid and imperious gesture over the young girl.

The latter started up, as if her system had received a powerful electric shock.

"His name ! I will it !" repeated Percival, for the third time.

"CAPTAIN RODOLPH !" replied the poor girl ; this last effort completely overpowering her, for she fell prostrate on the floor, without a sign of life or motion.

A few short moments were sufficient to restore Minna, and I then seriously interrogated her while she was asleep as to this personage. The young girl ordinarily very easily impressed, found great difficulty in replying to my question. At last, constrained by my will, she replied :

" 'This man is the son of Ralph Tryon.'

" 'His son !' I cried, surprised at this unexpected revelation. I then asked Minna why he wished us to be acquainted ? She replied that Tryon wished to perfect his son in knowledge, and that he knew he could obtain from me important information. She then suddenly exhibited great uneasiness, and added that I must be on my guard, that great danger threatened me—that she could not tell in what the danger consisted, but that it would emanate from the masked man and his father. More and more astonished, I pressed Minna to inform me why Tryon concealed from me his relationship with the masked man, and who Tryon really was—for I was satisfied that his name was an assumed one ? Minna made no reply. By no effort of mine, could I make her speak, although I tortured the poor girl by the force of my will. At last, breathless and exhausted, she begged for rest.

" ' I insist on your answering my questions,' I cried.

" ' I cannot,' replied Minna, writhing as if she were in a convulsion.

" ' Why ?'

" ' I cannot see. I cannot see.'

" ' What is necessary to make you see ?'

" ' I must be put in direct communication with those whose thoughts you wish me to know.'

" ' Then they must be here in the same room with you ?'

" ' Yes.'

" ' Is there no other means by which you can tell the thoughts of these men without seeing them ?'

" ' Yes, there is another method—'

" ' What is it ?'

" ' Give me something that has belonged to them—something they have worn—or what is still better, a lock of their hair.'

" ' A lock of hair !' I repeated, scarcely able to believe the assurance given me by the somnambulist. ' Is that all that is sufficient to know a person's thoughts—who he is—and where he is ?'

" ' Yes—if you command it.'

" A sudden idea entered my head—I remembered the lock of hair that I possessed, and I determined at once to try her powers. I placed it in her hands. At first she trembled and hesitated, and appeared to experience great difficulty in replying to my questions. But at length light appeared to break in upon her.

" ' The person from whom this lock of hair was cut, was very young at the time.'

" ' Yes,' I replied—' and now—'

" ' Now he is a man.'

" ' Do you see him ?'

" ' Perfectly, although he is a long way from here.'

" ' He is in this land.'

" ' No.'

" ' Indeed !' I exclaimed, in a tone of amazement, for I knew that the young man who had claimed to be Mr Mordent's son, was at that moment at Mordent Grange.

" ' He is not in any part of the country ?'

" ' No.'

" ' Where is he then ?'

" ' He is in the Indian Territory.'

" I was perfectly bewildered with surprise —Minna had never deceived me before—and yet I could scarcely believe what I heard. I interrogated her more closely. Her replies became more precise and clear. She entered into the most minute details as to the person she saw, and described the scenery where he was at that moment, with the most rigorous exactitude. And at last the name of Alfred and Eagle Eye escaped her lips."

" The names I bear !" cried the young man, who had been listening with the utmost attention to Mr Percival's story.

" Yes, your name," replied the elder traveller. " My doubts were now all dispelled, and I felt certain that the present occupant of Mordent Grange was an impostor. Three days afterwards I resumed the same interrogations—and received the same answers, varied only by your change of place. I determined to test her powers in another way, and fate befriended me, for a few days afterwards, I met the pretended Alfred Mordent, and pressed him to come and see me at my house. He accepted the invitation, and called the next day. I introduced Minna to him as my daughter. The beauty of the charming girl made an immediate impression on my visitor. Minna had studied the part she was to act, and while conversing with the young man, she fixed her eyes on a ring he wore on one of his fingers. The latter could not help noticing the earnest gaze, and he removed the ring, in order that she might examine it more easily. Minna took it, and playfully placed it on her own finger—she then handed it back with a half-sigh of regret. Our visitor asked my permission to present her with it. I thanked him, and permitted her to accept it."

" But what did you want the ring for ?" interrupted Alfred.

" Simply to obtain information about the donor. Do you not remember that it was necessary that Minna should possess some object worn by the person concerning whom she was to give me information ? The young man soon afterwards took his leave, asking permission to visit my house again. He 'had scarcely left the house before I put Minna to sleep, and interrogated her as to our visitor by means of the ring. She revealed the whole truth, and a terrible revelation it was. This man who had just left us—this man who had passed for the son of Henry and Catherine Mordent—this man was a wretch, a man of the most odious character— a robber of the worst kind. Suddenly Minna blushed and trembled. I interrogated her again.

" ' He loves me,' said she, in a heart-rending voice. ' You have ordained me to a life of trouble and woe by bringinging me in the presence of that man !'

" In answer to my further questions, she replied, that he who was called Alfred Mordent was the man I had met at Ralph Tryon's, and who she affirmed was his son.

I was thunderstruck at these revelations. What was I to believe? What was I to do? My mind, however, was soon made up. I determined that I would go and search for the rightful heir to the Mordent estates. I made the necessary arrangements that very day, and placing Minna in the care of a respectable family, I started off on my travels to the great West; and to-day, after three years of unremitting exertion, God has conducted me to you."

Mr Percival was silent, and appeared to be addressing a mute prayer to the Almighty. In a few minutes he resumed:

"And now, Alfred Mordent," said he, "you know your rights. The man who so basely assassinated your father, and who caused the death of your mother, in all probability yet lives. An impostor has seized upon your birthright. Answer, Alfred, what do you intend to do?"

Alfred leaped on his feet like a young chained lion, who suddenly breaks his bonds.

"What will I do?" he exclaimed—"what will I do? I will tell you—before God who hears us. In face of this immense solitude that surrounds us, in the presence of him who was my father's friend, I swear to find out my father's assassin, and to wash out the injury he has done me in his blood. I swear to consecrate my life, my strength, my intelligence, to this one end, and never to enter my father's house until this vow is accomplished."

"It is well," said Mr Percival; "I recognise in your words your father's character, as I recognise in your features a resemblance to your unfortunate mother. The oath you have made shall be kept. But there are great difficulties to be overcome. Your enemy is powerful; his position is a formidable one. The law has already decided in his favour, and material proofs are wanting to you. The scar on your left arm, although satisfactory to me, would not avail you much in a court of justice."

"I will surmount all these difficulties," cried Alfred, in a clear ringing voice.

"We will wait patiently, and act when the opportunity occurs. In the meantime, it will be necessary that we should return to civilised life. It will be better that you should appear there as my nephew. Your mother's name was Grantly; it will be better that you should take that. Let your name be for the present, Henry Grantly."

"Agreed," said Alfred, "I will trust everything to you. God who has preserved me through all the perils of an adventurous life will not now desert me."

Mr Percival wrapped his blanket round him, and threw himself all his length on the ground, and abandoned himself to his own thoughts. Alfred respected his companion's silence—but the news that he had heard filled his mind with active thoughts. He seemed to require some occupation to calm the fever of his brain. For some time he paced up and down on the green sward; then he replenished the fire, and again resumed his walking. He reflected on all he had heard, and repeated mentally everything told him by his father's old friend. Sometimes the young man's face was lighted up with joy, and then again an expression of despair would settle on his features.

"If this man is deceiving me," said he, and his hand convulsively grasped the hunting-knife he wore in his belt. "Or if he should deceive himself—if he is mad. What reliance is there to be placed in clairvoyance? Can I believe it? O, this man must be mad, and I am still more crazy to believe him."

And Alfred shook his head with an expression of doubt, and then he seemed to be indulging in a new train of thought.

"And yet," he continued—"while he spoke, the veil which enshrouded my brain appeared to be rent asunder—and memory seemed to be awakened. Yes, even at this moment, I can see that old house, and the mountains surrounding it—I remember—my mother snatching me up from my bed. Kate! Kate! yes, that was the name my father called her by. Port Clinton—Harrisburg—the Schuylkill—yes, everything is coming back vividly to my mind again."

The young man walked faster, as if the movement would aid his thoughts.

"That precipice—that gulf—I feel myself suspended there—a shock—wounds—yes, it must be true!"

Whilst Alfred was thus engaged, Mr Percival remained motionless on the ground. The young man stopped suddenly, and gazed on him for a minute without speaking.

"Perhaps he is mad," he murmured; "but evidently Providence has led him here, and I cannot deny his decrees. God often makes use of means which our poor human intelligence cannot comprehend. Besides, what have I to fear in following this man? My arm is strong, my hand is firm, and my eyes are clear. What have I to risk? I, a poor dweller of the prairie. My mind is made up —I *will* follow him."

----

## CHAPTER XIII.

### FURTHER REVELATIONS.

DURING a few moments which followed this terrible scene, and which evidently was only the prelude to a scene still more terrible, a profound silence reigned in the chamber. Tryon, Reynold, and Percival stood looking at each other with glaring eyes. The old man, with his features hideously distorted, his eyes bloodshot, and his lips half-open, was evidently a

www.ingramcontent.com/pod-product-compliance
Lightning Source LLC
Chambersburg PA
CBHW081502230626
47052CB00013B/1211